The First Incantation

Phoebe's heart pounded as she clutched *The Book of Shadows*. Maybe I should just put the book back, she thought.

But she couldn't. She had to read on.

"'Hear now the words of the witches,'" she chanted. "'The secrets we hid in the night.'"

A bolt of lightning shot through the sky, followed by the rumble of thunder.

Phoebe jolted upright. Could the incantation summon lightning and thunder? she wondered. She shook her head hard, trying to knock that crazy thought away.

She returned to the book. "'The oldest of gods are invoked here. The great work of magic is sought.'"

Lightning tore through the sky again. Then a strange light faintly glistened in the center of the room.

Phoebe laid her trembling hands on the ancient book. Had she somehow summoned this light by reading the incantation? What would happen if she finished it?

THE POWER OF THREE

A Novelization by Eliza Willard
Based on the hit TV series and teleplay
"Something Wicca This Way Comes"
Created by Constance M. Burge

A Parachute Press Book

POCKET PULSE

New York London Toronto Sydney Singapore

This book is a work of fiction. Names, characters, places and incidents are products of the author's imagination or are used fictitiously. Any resemblance to actual events or locales or persons, living or dead, is entirely coincidental.

An *Original* Publication of POCKET BOOKS

 POCKET PULSE published by
Pocket Books, a division of Simon & Schuster Inc.
1230 Avenue of the Americas, New York, NY 10020

™ © 1999 Spelling Television, Inc. All Rights Reserved.

ISBN: 0-671-04162-2

First Pocket Pulse printing November 1999

10 9 8 7 6 5 4 3 2

POCKET PULSE and colophon are trademarks of Simon & Schuster Inc.

Printed in the U.S.A.

THE POWER OF THREE

PROLOGUE

Serena Fredrick flipped open the white kitchen shutters and stared out into the night. Through the mist, lights glowed softly in the apartment building across the street, and gray clouds hid a full moon over the city of San Francisco. Her heart jumped as a flash of lightning pierced the sky. Thunder rumbled through the electric air and right through Serena's bones. Rain poured down onto the slick pavement below.

She nervously ran a pale hand through her shoulder-length blond hair. She sensed that something was wrong. The fine hairs on the back of her neck tingled. Someone was watching her—watching and waiting for her to lower her guard.

She had accepted her destiny as a good

witch long ago, yet she still shuddered at the thought of the evil that lurked in the underbelly of the city. She'd been fighting that evil for all of her twenty-eight years. For Serena lived in a world that few knew existed: the world of witches, warlocks, demons, and monsters. She shivered, wondering what form of evil might be hunting her now. There was so much to fear.

Serena shook her head. Stop being paranoid, she told herself. It's the storm that's making you so tense.

She opened a can of food for her cat and spooned it into a bowl. "Come on, baby!" she called, walking into the hallway.

The white Siamese Serena had adopted as her familiar stared at her with its jewel-like blue eyes. It purred as she placed the bowl on the hallway floor.

"Good girl," Serena said, stroking its back as it ate. She fingered the gold charm on her cat's collar—a full circle with three interlocking arcs inside. The triple link—the symbol of goodness. She had tattooed the same image underneath her collarbone for luck.

Another bolt of lightning brightened the room, followed by a crash of thunder. The lights in the apartment flickered off and on, and fear jolted through Serena's body once again. "A protective spell," she said softly. "For peace of mind."

Serena walked back into the kitchen, poured red wine into a silver chalice, and hurried into the living room. She placed the chalice on a low round table covered with a dark blue cloth. She kneeled next to the table, then glanced at the colorful arc of unlit candles, the bowl of herbs, and the ceremonial knife that rested on it.

She took a deep breath and gingerly touched the wick of the first candle in the arc with her index finger. "Fire," Serena whispered. A small flame emerged from her fingertip, lighting the candle. She touched another candle, and another, until they all burned brightly.

Serena closed her eyes and placed her palms together. For peace of mind, she reminded herself, then she opened her eyes and began her spell. "Ancient One of the earth so deep," she chanted, crossing her arms over her chest. "Master of moon and sun. I shield you in my Wiccan way, here in my circle round, asking you to protect this space, and offer your sun force down. . . ."

A slight breeze made the candles flicker.

Behind her Serena heard the nervous patter of her cat's feet suddenly bolting through the hallway. The hair prickled on the back of her neck again. Someone *was* watching her. She knew it. Someone was standing right behind her.

Serena gathered her courage and quickly

turned her head. She gasped when she saw a man hovering in the shadows of the room.

Who? she thought nervously. *Who is it?*

He stepped into the light with his hands behind his back, smiling.

A face I know, Serena thought. She let out a breath of relief. Thank goodness. "What are you doing here?" she asked him.

But her friend said nothing in return.

Serena rose to her feet and smiled, moving closer. "What's going on?"

Again, no reply.

Serena sensed that something was wrong as the man brought his hands out from behind his back. She gasped when she saw what he was hiding.

The long blade of a double-edged knife flashed in the candlelight. He tightly gripped the golden handle encrusted with red and blue stones.

Serena opened her mouth, but before she could speak, she felt the burning pain of the knife plunging into her stomach.

The crashing thunder drowned out Serena's screams, and she fell helplessly to the floor.

CHAPTER
1

"**Prue's going to kill me,**" Piper Halliwell muttered to herself. Her arms loaded with groceries, she rushed up the rain-slicked steps of the red-and-cream-colored Victorian house she shared with her older sister. She didn't know what time it was, but she knew she was late—*really* late.

Piper and Prue had been living in the old San Francisco house for about six months—ever since their grandmother died. Grams had willed the house to them and their younger sister, Phoebe, who was living in New York City. The three sisters loved the house and knew it well—they'd grown up in it, raised by Grams after their mother died when they were little. Their father hadn't been around to take care of them.

He'd never really kept in touch with them after the divorce.

Prue and Piper usually got along well, but Piper knew that one of her older sister's pet peeves—and she had many—was lateness. Piper tried her best to be punctual, but something always seemed to come up. She didn't know how Prue managed to keep her life so well under control.

Soaking wet, Piper burst through the front door. "Prue?" she called out.

"In here," Prue replied, "working on the chandelier."

Piper set the groceries on the foyer floor. She squeezed some water from her long, dark hair as she followed Prue's voice into the middle parlor.

Twenty-seven-year-old Prue was balanced on top of a ladder, fiddling with an ornate crystal chandelier. She smoothed the dark bangs of her shoulder-length bob with her fingers and sighed. Then she scowled at Piper, narrowing her ice blue eyes.

Piper leaned on the round wooden table underneath the chandelier. Prue was only two years older than Piper, but sometimes she treated Piper more like a child than a sister. Yup, Piper thought. Prue's pissed. "Sorry I'm late," she told her sister. "Really."

"What else is new?" Prue asked without even looking at her. "You were supposed to be here when the electrician came, Piper. I would have been here myself, but you know I can't leave the museum until six o'clock." She grimaced, trying to push a hanging wire out of sight.

"I know, I know," Piper replied. "But I was shopping in Chinatown, and then it started raining. . . . I guess I didn't realize how long I was gone." She moved from the table and peeled off her wet raincoat. "Did you fix the chandelier?"

"Not so far," Prue complained. "Hey, how did your interview go? Are you a real chef now?"

"Not yet," Piper replied. "The fabulous Chef Moore demands an audition. So I have to go back to the restaurant tomorrow and cook for him. Something unusual. 'Something worthy of me,' " Piper said, mimicking the chef's voice. " 'Something worthy of Quake.' "

"Quake?" Prue wrinkled her long, fine nose as if something smelled bad. "Is that what the restaurant is called?"

"Yeah. It's in North Beach. Very chic." Piper stepped into the hallway to hang up her raincoat on a coatrack.

"Oh, no!" Prue cried. Piper heard a small, tinkling crash. She hurried back into the middle parlor. A small crystal chandelier ornament lay smashed on the floor.

Prue glared at the tiny pile of glass, cursing.

Piper held back a smile. Something always seemed to be breaking in the old house, but she couldn't help but love the place.

Grams' antiques and oriental rugs still filled the spacious home. Old family photos lined the stairwell. The front door and the stair windows were made of green and yellow stained-glass squares. On sunny days, the light filtered softly through them, giving the house a warm glow.

Piper kicked at a shard of glass on the burnished-wood floor. "Don't worry, Prue," she said. "I'll get the dustpan and clean it up."

"Thanks," Prue said curtly. Piper could hear the exasperation in her voice. Prue hated it when things didn't run smoothly.

Piper started toward the kitchen to get the dustpan when the doorbell rang. She crossed the parlor and opened the door. Standing on the front porch was her boyfriend, Jeremy Burns. He carried a dozen red roses in one arm and a long, rectangular package, prettily wrapped and topped with a purple bow, in the other.

Well, Piper thought, eyeing Jeremy's rain-flattened hair and goofy grin. He certainly does look cute all wet from the rain—especially when he's carrying roses.

She wrapped her arms around his broad shoulders and kissed him, pulling him into the house. "What are you doing here? I thought you were investigating a story."

Jeremy flashed his boyish smile. He towered over Piper, handsome and tall, with wavy dark brown hair and warm hazel eyes. He waved to Prue, who was still working on the chandelier.

"Hi, Jeremy," Prue called from atop the ladder.

Jeremy offered the roses to Piper. "These are for you."

"What for?" she asked. She cradled the roses in her arms, trying not to show how pleased she was. Jeremy was spoiling her. Throughout the eight months they'd been seeing each other, he was always doing something sweet, and she never got tired of it.

"Do I need a reason?" he replied. "I just saw them and I thought you should have them." He kissed her softly on the cheek.

"You're so sweet, Jeremy. Thank you!" Piper self-consciously touched her cheek. She could practically feel it glowing.

"Well, I have to get back to work," Jeremy said, "but I want to give you one more thing first." He tapped a finger on the package. "I think this will help you out with your audition tomorrow."

Piper shook the package. "What is it?"

"You'll find out," Jeremy said with a grin. He glanced at his watch. "Got to run. I'm interviewing someone in ten minutes." He kissed her again. "Hope you like it," he called as he ran through the rain to his car.

Piper closed the front door and joined Prue back in the middle parlor.

"What's in the package?" Prue asked, climbing down from the ladder.

Piper placed the roses on the table. She tugged at the purple ribbon on the package and tore open the paper to reveal a wooden box. She slid open the top and pulled out a dark bottle with a white label. "This is great!" she cried, showing it to Prue.

Prue grabbed the bottle. "Jeremy gave you a bottle of port wine?" she asked.

"It's very special port," Piper explained. "The ultimate ingredient for my audition recipe." She pointed to the white label on the bottle. "This wine may just get me the job at Quake."

"Nice boyfriend," Prue admitted, handing the bottle back to Piper.

"Yeah, I know." Piper glanced at the label once more, then rested the bottle on the table. "I guess I should put my groceries in the fridge." Then she remembered the broken glass on the floor. Prue followed her eyes and guessed what she was thinking.

"That's okay," Prue said. "*I'll* clean up the glass."

Piper felt a little guilty as she walked into the foyer, grabbed the groceries and started toward the kitchen. Passing through the dining room, she noticed a shiny wooden board game on the table.

"I don't believe it," she said, setting everything down again. "Tell me that's *not* our old spirit board. I used to love that thing!"

"I found it in the basement while I was looking for the circuit box," Prue said, walking into the dining room.

Piper touched the antique spirit board gently. Mom gave this to us, she thought. Piper couldn't even remember the last time she and Prue and their younger sister, Phoebe, had played with it—it was so long ago.

The board was covered with letters, numbers, and symbols, and came with a pointer to spell out words. She and her sisters would lightly place their fingers on the pointer. The pointer was supposed to move by itself, guided by spirits, to spell out messages and answer their questions.

Prue always used to ask the board what she was going to be when she grew up, Piper remembered. Phoebe used to ask silly questions like, "What are we having for lunch today?"

And I would always ask when Prue and Phoebe would stop fighting, Piper thought. I never *did* get a straight answer, she remembered.

Piper picked up the board and flipped it over. She smiled as she read aloud the writing on the back, " 'To my three beautiful girls. May this give you the light to find the Shadows. The power of three will set you free. Love, Mom.' "

She turned to Prue. "We never figured out what this inscription meant."

"Well, I think we should send the board to Phoebe," Prue said with a laugh. "That girl is so in the dark, a little light might help. Maybe she can use it to figure out where Dad is. You never know. . . ."

Piper frowned. She couldn't believe that Prue was still ragging on their younger sister after all this time. "You're always so hard on Phoebe," she said.

"Piper, she has no vision," Prue complained. "No sense of the future."

"I really think she's coming around," Piper told her.

Prue threw up her hands. "Yeah, right. And that's why she went to New York to look for Dad. I mean, what's the point? The guy has been out of our life since forever. Who says he's even *in* New York?"

"You know that's not the real reason she left," Piper insisted. She eyed Prue carefully. Should I go any further? she wondered. Should I bring up Roger? That's why Phoebe really left San Francisco.

Prue had been engaged to Roger—until Phoebe announced that Roger had tried to seduce her. When Prue confronted Roger, he told her that it was Phoebe who had made a pass at *him*. Prue didn't know what to think. She broke up with Roger, but she blamed

Phoebe for the whole mess and never forgave her.

Piper believed Phoebe. She knew that her little sister would never try to steal Prue's fiancé. Phoebe was only trying to help Prue when she told her what a jerk Roger had been.

But Prue and Phoebe had never gotten along, and Prue refused to give Phoebe the benefit of the doubt.

"I don't care why she left," Prue said. "As long as she doesn't come back." She spun around and stomped through the foyer.

Piper chased after her. She had hoped that with a little time apart her two sisters would patch up their disagreements—at least enough so that Phoebe could move back home. Piper had been talking to Phoebe for months, and Phoebe was ready to make peace with Prue, especially since things hadn't worked out for her in New York. But Piper could see now that Prue was still angry, and had no intention of forgiving Phoebe.

"Prue!" Piper called. "Wait!"

Prue stopped in the middle parlor and whirled around. "What?" she demanded.

Piper bit her lip nervously. "Um, I have to tell you something, and, well . . . I don't think . . ."

Piper stopped and stared at her sister. How could she tell Prue that Phoebe was returning to San Francisco? Prue had made it clear that she didn't want Phoebe back in the house.

"What is it, Piper?" Prue asked again.

"You know how we've been talking about what to do with that spare room?" Piper asked.

Prue nodded.

"Well, I think you're right," Piper said. "Maybe we do need a roommate."

Prue glanced at the chandelier. "Maybe we can rent the room at a reduced rate in exchange for some help around the house. I'll put an ad in the *Chronicle*," she said, then headed into the living room.

"Phoebe's good with a wrench," Piper quickly replied, following her.

"Phoebe lives in New York," Prue said, glancing back at Piper.

"Uh . . ." Piper took a deep breath. "Not anymore," she blurted out.

Prue stopped and turned. "*What?*"

"I've wanted the three of us back together for a long time," Piper said. "And . . . well . . . Phoebe's left New York. She's moving back in with us."

Prue groaned. "You've *got* to be kidding."

"Well, I could hardly say no," Piper said. "It's her house, too. Grams left it to all three of us."

"Months ago," Prue added. "And we haven't seen or spoken to her since!"

Piper folded her arms across her chest.

"Well, *you* haven't spoken to her," she told Prue.

"No, I haven't," Prue replied. "Look, maybe you've forgotten why I'm still mad at her?"

"No, of course not," Piper said, trying to calm Prue down. "But Phoebe has nowhere else to go. She lost her job. She's in debt. . . ."

"And this is *news?* How long have you known about this, anyway?" Prue demanded.

"A-a couple of days," Piper stammered. "Maybe a week—or two."

"Thanks for sharing, Piper." Prue glared at her. "When does she arrive?"

Why does Prue have to be so difficult? Piper thought as the front door burst open, and Phoebe entered the foyer.

Piper smiled at Phoebe, then glanced back at Prue. "Um, she arrives now, okay?"

CHAPTER
2

Surprise!" Phoebe said, holding up a key. "I found the hide-a-key and let myself in."

Prue stared at her youngest sister as she hung up her dripping umbrella on the hook by the front door and plopped her wet backpack on the floor. Just seeing Phoebe brought back bad memories, not only of Roger, but of the horrible fights the two of them had when they were younger.

Prue was always bailing Phoebe out of some kind of mess, but that didn't stop Phoebe from getting herself into even more trouble. Phoebe never considered the consequences of her actions, and Prue was sick of cleaning up the messes Phoebe left behind.

Piper was constantly trying to patch things

up between Prue and Phoebe, but after this last incident with Roger, Prue was convinced Piper's efforts were futile.

Prue didn't think she could ever forgive Phoebe, not this time.

Deep down, Prue didn't want to believe that Phoebe had come on to her ex-fiancé, but what else could she think? What was Phoebe doing in Roger's apartment? Phoebe's excuse was so lame: He tricked her into going there. Yeah, right.

"Phoebe!" Piper crossed the room and threw her arms around her. "Welcome home."

"Hello, Piper." Phoebe hugged her sister back. She glanced at Prue over Piper's shoulder and gave her a shy smile.

Prue had to admit that Phoebe looked good. Her new chin-length haircut suited her, and her figure was in great shape, as usual. She wore jeans and a tank top but no raincoat, and of course, Prue noticed.

Why is she here? Prue wondered. What does she want from us?

"It's so good to see you!" Piper told Phoebe. Then she turned to Prue. "Isn't it, Prue?"

"I'm speechless," Prue muttered. I hope Phoebe doesn't expect us to sell Grams' house just because she's in debt, she thought. I bet that's why she came back. She needs money. Prue crossed her arms in front of her chest. Well, Phoebe's in for a big disappointment. There's no way we're giving up the house.

A car horn beeped outside.

"Oops. I forgot about the cab," Phoebe said.

"Why am I not surprised?" Prue replied.

"I'll take care of it," Piper offered. She grabbed Prue's bag off the foyer table and opened the door.

"Hey, that's *my* purse!" Prue called out, but it was too late. Piper was already halfway to the cab.

"Thanks, Prue. I'll pay you back," Phoebe promised.

Prue nodded, but she wasn't going to hold her breath waiting. Phoebe had never paid back a loan in her life.

Prue pointed to the backpack Phoebe had set on the floor. "Is that all you brought?" she asked in an effort to make conversation.

"It's all I own," Phoebe admitted. "That and a bike, but I left that here, remember?"

Prue glanced nervously around the room, not knowing what else to say. She felt uncomfortable. What was taking Piper so long?

"Look, Prue," Phoebe began. "I know you don't want me here—"

"We're not selling Grams' house," Prue blurted out.

"Is that why you think I came back?" Phoebe asked.

"The only reason Piper and I gave up our

apartment and moved back here," Prue replied, "was because this house has been in our family for generations—"

"No history lesson needed," Phoebe interrupted her. "I grew up here, too, you know." She sighed. "Now can we talk about what's *really* bothering you?"

"No," Prue said as calmly as she could. "I'm still furious with you."

"So you'd rather have a tense reunion filled with boring chitchat and unimportant small talk?" Phoebe asked with a smirk.

"No," Prue replied. "But otherwise we won't have anything to talk about."

"I never touched Roger," Phoebe said. "I know you don't believe me because of what that Armani-wearing, wine-slugging, trust-fund jerk told you, but—"

"Hey!" Piper said, sounding a little too cheerful as she returned through the front door. "I have a great idea. What do you say I whip up a fabulous reunion dinner?"

A flash of lightning suddenly sliced the sky and made the lights flicker.

Prue glanced at Piper and then glared at Phoebe. "I'm not hungry."

"I ate on the bus." Phoebe crossed the foyer, grabbed her backpack, and stomped up the stairs.

"Okaaaay," Piper said. "We'll have the group hug later. How does that sound?"

"You got it." Prue wheeled around and marched into the kitchen. She felt as though she was about to explode. Why did Phoebe have to come back to San Francisco just when things were getting back to normal? She was finally getting over Roger. It was a little weird working with him at the museum, but otherwise her job was going really well.

Prue grabbed hold of the counter and took a deep breath. Get it under control, she coaxed herself. Just pull yourself together.

Phoebe sat on her bed in a baby blue T-shirt and plaid pajama bottoms, not really watching the small television on top of her dresser. Instead, she was thinking about her oldest sister.

Phoebe was a bit surprised that Prue was still so angry with her. Six months was a long time to hold a grudge—even for Prue. But what hurt more was that Prue still thought the whole mess with Roger was Phoebe's fault.

Maybe it *was* my fault, Phoebe said to herself. After all, I shouldn't have been so gullible when Roger asked me to come up to his apartment to pick up something for Prue. I should have known that there wasn't any package— that he just wanted to get me up there to seduce me. She shuddered, as she remembered Prue catching them together just as she was pushing Roger away.

It wasn't my fault, she reminded herself.

Roger was a jerk for coming on to me. It's better that Prue knows what he's really like, even if she winds up hating me for the rest of my life.

It had been hard for Phoebe to come home, knowing she had to face Prue. The least Prue could do was make a little effort, Phoebe thought. At least try to understand.

Phoebe shook her head. She didn't want to think about it anymore. Prue was never going to change. Phoebe tried to focus on the newscast on the television when she heard a knock at the bedroom door. She got up and opened it.

Piper lounged in the doorway, dressed for bed in a short cotton nightgown and silk kimono. "Hungry, Phebes?" she asked, offering up a wicker tray with sandwiches, carrot sticks, and two glasses of iced tea.

Piper carefully set the wicker tray on the bed. She picked up a glass and took a sip of the iced tea. "I'm sure Prue will come around," she assured Phoebe.

"I don't think so. Not this time." Phoebe grabbed a turkey sandwich. "Prue's pretty angry. I should have stayed in New York." She took a tiny bite of the sandwich. "Why didn't you tell her I was coming home?"

"And give her a chance to change the locks?" Piper said. "I don't think so. Besides, *you* should have told her, not me."

"Good point." Phoebe took another bite of her

sandwich. "It's just so hard to talk to her. She's always been more like a mother than a sister."

"That's not her fault," Piper said. "She practically had to sacrifice—"

"—Her own childhood to help raise us," Phoebe finished. She'd heard that a million times before. "Yeah, yeah, yeah."

"Hey, we're lucky she was so responsible," Piper went on. "You and I had it easy. She took care of everything. We didn't have much to worry about."

"Yeah, well, I'm twenty-two years old now. I don't need her to be my mom anymore. I need her to be my sister." Phoebe picked up a carrot stick. "I'm sick of talking about Prue. Let's talk about you. What's going on? How's your love life?"

Piper grinned shyly. "Well, as a matter of fact . . ." She twisted a strand of dark hair around one finger. "It's great!"

"Really?" Phoebe sat up. Now, here was something to talk about. "Tell me everything!"

"Well, I'm still with Jeremy," Piper said. "I told you about him. He's a reporter for the *Chronicle*, and he's adorable!"

"Just adorable?" Phoebe asked.

Piper blushed. "More than that," she replied. "He's got—he's got these *eyes*, you know?"

Phoebe laughed. "Wow, he's got *eyes*, huh? That's something special."

Piper poked Phoebe in the arm. "You know

what I mean. He's like, the most incredible guy I've ever met. At first I couldn't believe he was even interested in me."

"How could he *not* be interested in you, Piper?" Phoebe said. "When did you meet him?"

"About six months ago—right before Grams died," Piper told her. "We met in the hospital cafeteria the day she was admitted. He was covering a story. I was bawling over a bagel. He handed me a napkin."

"How romantic." Phoebe rolled her eyes.

"Actually it was. The napkin had his phone number on it." Piper paused. "Jeremy was really there for me while Grams was sick, Phoebe. Really, he's always there for me." Piper looked away and blushed. "I think he might be, you know, *the one*," she confided.

"Wow," Phoebe breathed. "That's incredible. I'm so happy for you!" She leaned over the wicker tray to hug Piper. Phoebe really was glad to see Piper so happy. Piper had always defended her. At least I'm close to *one* of my sisters, Phoebe thought.

Piper suddenly pulled away. She smiled, and pointed at the TV screen. "There he is! That's Jeremy!"

Phoebe grabbed the remote control and turned up the volume. A female reporter at a crime scene was describing the grisly murder of a woman. A tall, sexy-looking guy with broad shoulders lingered in the background, talking to the police.

"*That's* Jeremy?" she asked Piper. "He's gorgeous."

"He must be working on this story," Piper said.

"The killer may be targeting women who are members of some kind of cult," the news reporter said. "Each of the three victims had the same tattoo under her collarbone."

A picture of an elaborate tattoo flashed on the screen: three arcs interlocked inside a circle.

Phoebe watched the report, and began to worry. "Did you know about this?" she asked Piper. "How long has this psycho been out there?"

"Shh!" Piper said, waving her hand at Phoebe.

"The woman's body was found beside what looked to be some kind of altar," the reporter continued. "Another indication that a cult may be involved."

"People are getting weirder and weirder in San Francisco," Piper said when the report was over. "We have to be careful—especially since this crazy guy is on the loose."

"Knock, knock."

Phoebe turned her eyes to the door.

Prue stood at the threshold carrying a down comforter.

"This was always the coldest room in the

house," Prue said, dropping the comforter on a chair by the door.

Suddenly Phoebe felt the mood of the room turn tense. Prue stood in the doorway, not moving.

It's as if she thinks something horrible will happen to her if she comes in here, Phoebe thought. "Thanks, Prue," she said without a smile.

Piper sat quietly beside her—probably trying to figure out what to say, Phoebe thought. Some perfect words that will magically draw Prue and me back together.

Prue gave Phoebe a slight nod, then stared at her for a moment.

Is Prue going to say something to me? Phoebe wondered. Maybe she's not as angry as I thought. Will we actually have a sister-to-sister talk?

Phoebe was totally willing. In fact, it was something she'd wanted from Prue practically her whole life. She'd give anything if Prue would only open up to her—anything in the world.

But Prue didn't say another word. She turned on her heel and left.

Phoebe stared at Prue's back as she headed down the hall. I'll never understand it, she said to herself. Prue and I are sisters. How can we be so different?

Piper touched her arm. "Don't worry about

her," she said. "Prue just needs a little time to get used to things, okay?"

Phoebe frowned as she watched Prue head down the elaborate wooden staircase. Yeah, right, Phoebe thought. Who ever heard of sisters having to get used to each other? She didn't want to accept it, but she had to. She and Prue would never be close.

"Hey, I've got an idea," Piper said.

Phoebe groaned. "Another one of your great ideas?"

"It *is* a great idea," Piper insisted. "And I think it will cheer you up. Come on." Piper grabbed Phoebe's hand and dragged her down the creaky stairs.

"Where are we going?" Phoebe demanded.

"To the living room," Piper replied. "I've got a surprise for you. You're going to love it."

Phoebe plopped down on the living room couch. "I'll be right back," Piper promised.

Phoebe spotted an old, framed photograph on the coffee table. She reached over and picked it up. The picture showed Prue, Piper, and Phoebe as little girls, with their arms around one another, smiling.

I wish it could be like that again, Phoebe thought. Like the old days. All of us happy— happier, anyway.

Piper returned, carrying something. "Look!" she cried. "Our old spirit board!"

"Where did you find this?" Phoebe took

the board from Piper. Just a touch of the smooth old wood brought back childhood memories.

"Prue found it in the basement. Let's try it out," Piper suggested. "Just for fun."

"Why not?" Phoebe placed the game on the coffee table. Then she jumped up and grabbed some candles off the sideboard. "Got any matches?"

Piper opened a drawer, pulled out a pack of matches, and tossed them to Phoebe. "I'll go find Prue. Maybe she wants to play," she said, hurrying from the room.

Phoebe set the candles on the coffee table and lit them. For atmosphere, she thought with a giggle.

Piper returned after a few minutes. "Prue's in the kitchen, making tea. She said she doesn't feel like playing right now."

"Surprise, surprise," Phoebe cracked.

Piper sat down on the couch. "Okay," she said. "What should we ask the spirits?"

"Hmmm . . ." Phoebe thought for a minute. "How about—What are we having for breakfast tomorrow?"

Piper laughed. "Come on, Phoebe. Ask a real question."

"All right." Phoebe closed her eyes to think. There were so many things she wanted to know about the future, but she decided to start with something practical.

"Let's ask it if I'll get a decent job in San Francisco," she said.

"All right." Piper moved the pointer to the center of the board. She and Phoebe set their fingers lightly on the pointer.

"Will I get a good job in San Francisco?" Phoebe asked the spirits, then glanced at Piper, who was staring at the board. Phoebe smiled to herself. Then she made the pointer quiver. "It's working!" she cried.

"You're pushing it!" Piper said. "You used to always push the pointer."

"I am not pushing it," Phoebe said with a grin. Then she made the pointer jet to the corner of the board where the word yes was printed. "Yes! It said yes!" Phoebe cried.

Piper took her fingers off the pointer. "Phoebe, I know you pushed it," she said. "I'm going to make some popcorn."

"Wait!" Phoebe called as Piper headed toward the kitchen. "What do you want me to ask the spirit board while you're gone?"

Piper stopped a moment. "How about asking it if Prue will sleep with someone other than herself this year?"

"That's a very important question," Phoebe said. "Maybe that's what's making Prue so cranky." She turned back to the spirit board. "Please say yes," she whispered as she touched the pointer. "Please . . . say . . . yes."

Suddenly the pointer zipped across the board and stopped at the letter A.

Phoebe gasped and pulled her hands away from the board as if it was burning hot. What's going on? I didn't push the pointer that time. I hardly touched it!

"Piper," she called out, a little scared.

The pointer zipped to the letter T.

Phoebe stared at it, amazed. No one was touching it now. It was moving by itself.

Phoebe's heart began to race. "Piper, get in here!" she cried.

"What?" Piper demanded, coming in from the kitchen.

"What did you guys do now?" Prue asked as she entered the living room, too.

Phoebe nervously scanned her sisters' faces. "The pointer on the spirit board," she told them. "It—it moved on its own."

Piper rolled her eyes, and Prue shot her a stinging "yeah, right" look.

"I'm serious," Phoebe insisted. "It spelled out A-T."

"That's because you pushed it," Piper said.

"You always used to move the pointer," Prue added.

"No," Phoebe said. "I didn't this time."

Prue put her hand on her hip. "I don't have time for this." She began to turn away.

"Prue—wait!" Phoebe cried. "My fingers weren't even touching the pointer—I swear!"

To Phoebe's surprise, Prue stopped. She didn't lose the skeptical expression on her face, but she didn't leave the room.

"Just watch it—it will move."

Come on, Phoebe thought as she stared at the pointer. Move! Move! I saw you do it before! But the pointer stayed where it was.

"This isn't funny, Phoebe," Prue said. "It isn't even entertaining."

Piper and Prue started to leave. As soon as their backs were turned, the pointer quickly jerked to the bottom of the board, then back to the letter T.

"Ah, ah, ah!" Phoebe cried out, surprised. "It did it again! It moved!"

Piper and Prue stopped. Prue walked over to the spirit board. She glanced at it and frowned. "It's still on the letter T, Phoebe."

"I swear it moved!" Phoebe yelled.

"Sure it did." Prue turned and left the room.

Phoebe watched in shock as the pointer slowly glided across the board again. She jumped from her chair. "It's doing it again!"

This time the pointer rested on the letter I.

Piper stared at the spirit board, her mouth open.

"You saw that, right?" Phoebe asked Piper.

"I—I think so, yeah," Piper replied.

"I told you I wasn't touching it," Phoebe said. She gestured toward the moving pointer. "Look!"

This time it stopped on the letter C.

Piper gasped. "Um, Prue, I think you'd better come back," she called nervously.

Phoebe quickly picked up an envelope and a pen from the coffee table and scribbled the letters the spirit board had spelled out.

Prue stormed into the living room. "Now what?" she asked.

"I think it's trying to tell us something," Phoebe replied. She held up the envelope with a shaky hand. "Attic."

CHAPTER
3

Attic?" Prue asked. "What kind of game are you playing, Phoebe?"

Phoebe swallowed hard. She didn't know how to explain it to Prue. It was so hard to believe, but it was true. The spirit board had sent them a message!

Thunder rumbled through the walls of the house. Phoebe gasped as the lights flickered and went out. Lightning flashed brightly for a moment, casting the living room in an eerie glow. When it disappeared, the house was completely dark, except for the few glimmering candles surrounding the spirit board.

Piper clung onto Prue's arm. "It's not a game. I saw the pointer move. I'm scared." She ran into the foyer and grabbed her raincoat.

"I'm going to Jeremy's house. And if you two are smart, you'll come with me."

Prue and Phoebe followed Piper into the parlor. Prue grabbed the raincoat from Piper's hand.

"Don't you think you're overreacting?" Prue asked.

"Yeah," Phoebe agreed. "Let's just go to the attic and look around a little."

"Don't you dare, Phoebe!" Piper cried. "We don't know what's up there. The electricity is out, and there's a killer on the loose. We've got to get out of here!"

Prue touched Piper's shoulder. "Don't worry," she assured her. "No one's going to the attic. But there's no point in leaving the house. We're perfectly safe here."

"Don't say that!" Piper cried. She took her coat back from Prue. "In horror movies, the person who says that is always the next to die."

"Piper, it's pouring rain out," Prue continued. "Look, I'm sure there's nothing in the attic, but we'll call a handyman tomorrow and have him check it out, okay? Besides Jeremy's not even home."

"So, I'll—I'll wait in the cab until he gets back from work," Piper replied.

Phoebe rummaged through the drawer in the parlor table and found a flashlight. She was frightened, too, but she wasn't going to ignore the message from the spirit board. It has to mean something, she thought. I have to find out what's up there.

"I'm going up to the attic," Phoebe announced. "Are you coming with me?"

Her sisters didn't seem to hear her.

Piper slipped on her raincoat. "Prue, I saw that pointer move."

"No." Prue firmly placed her hands on Piper's shoulders. "You saw Phoebe's fingers pushing the pointer. There's nothing in that attic. She's playing a joke on us."

Thanks for believing me, Prue, Phoebe thought. Not that I expected anything different from you.

Piper shook her head. "We don't know that. We've lived in this house for months now, and we've never been able to get the attic door open."

Prue turned to Phoebe. "Piper is freaking out. Will you please tell her it was all a joke?"

Phoebe shook her head. "I know it's hard to believe the pointer moved by itself," she told her sister, "but why would I lie about something like this?"

Piper quickly crossed the parlor to the cordless phone. She picked up the receiver and placed it to her ear. "Great. Now the phone doesn't work!" she cried.

"Yeah, the power's out," Prue reminded her. "Look, just go with me to the basement. Hold the flashlight while I check out the main circuit box."

"I don't want to go to the basement. Phoebe will go with you," Piper said quickly. "Won't you, Phoebe?"

Phoebe held up the flashlight. She wasn't going anywhere with Prue. "Nope," she replied. "I'm going to the attic."

"No, you're not," Prue said quickly. "We already agreed—"

"I am *not* waiting for some handyman to check out the attic," Phoebe told her. "And I'm certainly not going to wait until tomorrow. I'm going now."

She flicked on her flashlight and started up the stairs. But with each step she climbed, Phoebe grew more and more nervous. It was so dark and quiet up there. She heard only the raindrops beating on the roof, mimicking the rhythm of her heart. She began to have second thoughts. As unbelievable as it seemed, she was convinced that a spirit had sent her a message through the spirit board.

But what kind of spirit? Phoebe wondered. And what will I find in the attic?

She paused at the top of the stairs, shining her flashlight on the attic door. There it was. In all the years she'd lived in this house, she'd never been inside the attic.

An old dresser stood on the landing next to the door. On the floor beside it was a box full of junk.

Phoebe slowly reached for the door handle. She twisted the doorknob, but it didn't move. She rattled the knob and pushed on the door to no avail.

It's locked, she realized. Maybe I can jimmy it open somehow.

She opened the top drawer of the dresser and shined the flashlight inside. A rusty old nail file lay forgotten at the bottom of the drawer. She snatched it up and slid it between the door and the door frame, trying to pry the lock open.

It still wouldn't budge. Frustrated, Phoebe threw the nail file on the floor.

I guess Prue was right, she thought. We *will* need to call a handyman. There's no way to open that door.

Phoebe turned to go back downstairs, defeated. Then a soft creaking noise behind her made her stop. Her heart raced. What was that? she wondered nervously.

She slowly turned around and saw the attic door swing open—by itself.

Phoebe swallowed hard. The door had been securely locked—she was sure of it. It's another sign, she thought, another message from the spirit.

Frightened, Phoebe hesitated at first, then she stepped toward the door and peered into the dark room. "Hello?" she whispered. "Is anyone here?"

No one answered. She flashed her light around the room. She saw an old yellow chair, a dresser, a few lamps, some clothes . . . no sign of a psycho killer, she told herself. It was safe to go inside. Right?

Phoebe wasn't so sure. Suddenly she wished that Piper were with her—or even Prue.

Stop being such a chicken, she told herself. There's nothing scary up here. Just think of what Prue would say if you came running down the stairs like a little baby.

Phoebe mustered her courage. She had to go inside the attic—alone.

She cautiously entered the room, one slow step at a time. "Hello? Is anyone there?" she asked again.

She heard a noise from above, and her heart jumped. She flashed her light up at the peaked roof.

Nothing.

The only sound she heard now was the rain beating against the tall stained-glass windows on the far wall. A bolt of lightning flashed through the window. The room returned to darkness, except for Phoebe's flashlight.

Then, outside the window, she saw a strange, bright, steady glow.

That isn't lightning, Phoebe realized as the glow brightened. It looked more like a sunbeam than a flash of light. But it's nighttime. It couldn't be the sun, Phoebe reasoned, or even the moon. It's raining and the city is shrouded in fog.

She stared curiously at the strange light as it streamed through the window, illuminating the room. It beamed like a spotlight on an old trunk, which was set apart from all the other things in the attic.

Phoebe felt herself drawn to the trunk as if it was calling to her. She crossed the room to gaze at its intricately carved lid.

What's inside? she wondered. Could this be why the spirit board sent me up here? She took a deep breath. "Only one way to find out," she murmured.

She placed her flashlight on a shelf and kneeled on the floor in front of the trunk. The hinges creaked as she carefully lifted its dusty lid.

The strange beam of light glimmered through the window, and into the trunk. It was nearly empty, except for a large book resting at the bottom.

Phoebe lifted the book from a pile of dust and cobwebs. It's heavy, she thought as she tucked it under her arm and closed the lid of the trunk. Then she took her flashlight from the shelf, sat on top of the trunk, and gazed at what she had found.

The book, covered in brown leather, looked ancient. Phoebe blew the dust from the cover and brushed it with her hand. An exotic insignia was imprinted on the leather—three arcs interlocked inside a circle.

Phoebe stared at the insignia with a jolt of recognition. She knew that she'd seen a symbol like this somewhere before.

She shivered as the answer came to her. It's the same insignia I saw on the news tonight, she realized. The woman who was murdered had this tattooed under her collarbone!

Phoebe opened the ancient book and gazed at the first page. " 'The Book of Shadows,' " she read softly, feeling another chill travel through her body. "What is this?"

She tightly gripped the flashlight as she stared at the title page. It was written in ornate calligraphy, with the B and the S illustrated like letters in a medieval manuscript.

The Book of Shadows. Phoebe concentrated on the words. Then the title rang a bell inside her head. The spirit board, she remembered. Her mother had written on the back: "May this give you the light to find the Shadows."

And it had, Phoebe realized. The spirit board had pointed her to the attic.

Could this have been Mom's book? Phoebe wondered. She didn't really remember anything about her mother. She had died when Phoebe was just a toddler. Phoebe glanced back at the odd engraving on the cover. Was Mom somehow connected to those women who were murdered? she wondered. They all had tattoos of this symbol. Phoebe shook her head. How could Mom have anything to do with a cult?

Now Phoebe was more curious about the book than ever. She flipped through pages to an illustration—a woodcut picture of three women sleeping. Very old, Phoebe thought, studying the medieval-looking clothes and furniture in the picture.

She turned the page and found another old woodcut. This one showed three women, battling several horrible-looking beasts.

The next page pictured the women gathered in a circle, dancing and singing.

They could be a coven of witches, Phoebe thought. Are these women casting some kind of spell? Is this a book of witchcraft?

A crash of thunder made Phoebe jump. What am I doing here? she wondered. Her heart pounded as she clutched *The Book of Shadows*. Maybe I should just put the book back, she thought, and forget I ever found it.

But she couldn't. She knew this book had something to do with her mother, and she had to find out what it was. Besides, she was drawn to the book. She didn't know why, but she sensed that it held a clue to her destiny—the answer to the lost, floundering feeling she'd had for the last couple of years. She had to read on.

She turned another page to find a picture of

a scroll twisting around a pole. Next to it were words beautifully penned in colored ink and decorated with gold.

It looks like an incantation, Phoebe thought. She took a breath and began to read it out loud.

" 'Hear now the words of the witches,' " she chanted. " 'The secrets we hid in the night.' "

A bolt of lightning shot through the sky, followed by the rumble of thunder.

Phoebe jolted upright, then shrank away from the book. Could the words of the incantation summon lightning and thunder? she wondered. She shook her head hard, trying to knock that crazy thought away.

She returned to the book, reading it aloud. " 'The oldest of gods are invoked here. The great work of magic is sought.' "

Lightning tore through the sky again. Phoebe heard an especially sharp *crack!* just outside the house.

She whirled around to glance out the window. A burning branch, struck by lightning, fell off a tree and smashed on the ground.

Shaking, she turned away from the window and saw a strange light faintly glistening in the center of the room. She couldn't figure out where the glow was coming from. It seemed to have no source.

She steadied her trembling hands. This was Mom's book. Mom would not have been into anything bad, she tried to convince herself as she watched the strange light shimmer. It was amazing, yet frightening at the same time. Is it real? she wondered. Or is it some kind of phenomenon related to the storm?

Phoebe laid her hands on the ancient book. Had she somehow summoned this light by reading the incantation? What would happen if she finished it?

She had to find out.

She took a deep breath and read. " 'In this night and in this hour, I call upon the Ancient Power!' "

A draft blew through the room. The glow brightened.

" 'Bring your powers to we sisters three," she chanted, her voice shaking. "We want the power. Give us . . . the power!' "

With those words, the icy draft transformed into a wind. It blew around the attic, around Phoebe, around the table, swirling around and around like a tornado. Starry sparkles of light twinkled in the whirlwind, glowing intensely.

Phoebe's hair flew across her face. She sat perfectly still, clutching the book.

She wasn't shaking anymore. Her body felt strangely calm, tranquil. But her mind whirled like the mystical wind around her.

She glanced down at her lap, at the ancient book that sat there. "It's a book of witchcraft," she murmured. "I read it out loud, and I've unleashed something powerful. Maybe something horrible."

Phoebe sat in the center of the whirlwind, mesmerized, staring at the book's pages as they riffled in the swirling gusts.

Oh no, she thought, watching the pages fly. What have I done?

CHAPTER
4

Prue grabbed Piper by the hand and dragged her up the stairs toward the attic. "Phoebe's been up there a long time," she said. "I'm worried."

The beam of the flashlight bounced along the walls, casting an eerie glow on the photographs that hung there. The faces in the old portraits seemed to come alive in the shadows.

"First you make me go to the basement, now the attic," Piper complained. "There's a thunderstorm outside. The electricity's off. The phone doesn't work." She shuddered. "This is one creepy night."

Prue gripped Piper's hand tighter and continued up the stairs. She wished that she could calm her sister down, but she knew that Piper was easily freaked out. "Come on," Prue said. "We have to see if Phoebe's okay."

Prue stopped at the top of the stairs and shined the flashlight at the attic door.

"Amazing," Prue gasped. "She got it open."

She stepped inside the attic, beaming the flashlight around the room. Everything was quiet and still. Phoebe was sitting on an old wooden trunk, a book open in her lap.

"What are you doing?" Prue demanded.

Phoebe glanced up. She looked dazed.

"I'm . . . um . . . reading," she stammered, "an incantation."

She closed the book and held it out to Prue. "It was in this *Book of Shadows*," she explained. "I found it inside the trunk."

"Let me see that." Prue took the book and studied its cover. Then she opened it and flipped through the pages.

"Phoebe, how did you get in here?" Piper asked.

"The door, opened," Phoebe said.

Prue glanced at her sister. There was something different about Phoebe, but she couldn't put her finger on exactly what it was.

"Wait a minute," Piper said nervously. "You were reading an incantation? What kind of incantation?"

Prue half-listened to her sisters' conversation as she paged through the heavy book.

"It said something about there being three

essentials of magic," Phoebe spoke slowly, as if in a trance. "Feeling, timing, and the phases of the moon. If we were ever going to do this, now—midnight on a full moon—is the most powerful time."

Okay, Prue thought. Now Phoebe's really lost it.

"Do what?" Piper asked. "What are you talking about?"

"Receive our powers," Phoebe said, staring into space.

"What powers?" Piper cried. Her voice crackled with tension. "You included me in this?"

Prue quickly flipped to the front of the book, to the incantation that Phoebe was talking about. She gasped when she read the words. Phoebe has always been a flake, Prue said to herself, but I never thought that she would mess with this stuff.

"She included *all* of us," Prue told Piper, and read from *The Book of Shadows*. " 'Bring your powers to we sisters three.' " She held the book up for Piper to see. "It's a book of witchcraft."

"I can explain," Phoebe said. "Sort of."

"First it was the belly-dancing lessons," Prue interrupted her. "Then you got your navel pierced. Now you're going to be a witch? Give me a break." She handed the book to Piper and headed out the attic door. She wasn't going to hang around and listen to any more of Phoebe's nonsense.

"Spirit boards," Prue muttered, walking downstairs. "Books of witchcraft. It figures all of this freaky stuff would start when you arrived, Phoebe."

"Hey, I wasn't the one who found the spirit board," Phoebe blinked hard, snapping out of her daze. "You did."

"But it wasn't my fingers sliding around on the pointer," Prue shot back.

"It doesn't matter," Piper said. "Because nothing happened, right, Phoebe? When you read that incantation, nothing happened?"

Phoebe shrugged. "Well, my head spun around, and I vomited split-pea soup. How should I know?"

Prue didn't believe in witchcraft or incantations, and she didn't think Phoebe had done any harm. But she hoped that her sister wasn't going to get into this occult stuff just because she found some stupid book in the attic. Grams probably bought it at a yard sale or something. She was always collecting strange, old objects.

When they reached the ground floor, Prue glanced around the house, shining her flashlight in every dark corner. Nothing had changed. She was sure of it.

Piper paused at the bottom of the stairs. "Everything *looks* the same."

"Unfortunately," Prue joked, "the house still needs a ton of work."

"Everything *feels* the same," Piper added, looking around some more. "So nothing's changed. Right?"

"Of course nothing has changed," Prue insisted.

The old chandelier in the parlor suddenly flickered on.

"Hey! The lights!" Piper cried.

Prue stared at the chandelier, surprised. It's working. How could that be?

"You actually managed to fix the chandelier?" Piper asked.

"I—I didn't think so," Prue stammered. She hadn't done anything to the light, just touched a few wires. "I don't know what happened."

Phoebe put an arm around each of her sisters. "Maybe," she said, "just *maybe* it was—"

"Give me a break," Prue cut in. "It was *not* magic. There's probably a short in a wire and it will blow out any minute." At least that was what Prue hoped would happen. She liked to have a logical explanation for things, and a working chandelier that had been broken for months couldn't be explained any other way.

Phoebe glanced up at the sparkling chandelier and shrugged. "Whatever you say, Prue. Whatever you say."

*   *   *

Phoebe lay in bed that night, trying to sleep. It felt strange to be back in San Francisco again, stranger still to be back in the old house. She knew that something had occurred in the attic that night, something very important.

But she didn't want to talk to Prue and Piper about it. She couldn't. They'd never believe it.

Phoebe closed her eyes and tried to drift off to sleep. It had been a long day, and she'd just spent a week traveling by bus across the country. She should be exhausted, yet she couldn't stop thinking about *The Book of Shadows*.

She knew that she should be frightened, remembering the light and the wind gusting in circles around her. But for some reason she wasn't scared at all. In fact, she wanted to run right up to the attic to read *The Book of Shadows* from cover to cover. There was so much that she wanted to know. The book seemed to be calling her, tugging at her.

She tried to stop thinking about it. It's late, she told herself. I'll read it tomorrow. But as soon as she closed her eyes, the image of the strange symbol imprinted on the cover of the book flashed into her mind.

I'll never get any rest until I read it, Phoebe decided. She pushed off the covers and got out of bed. She grabbed the flashlight off her nightstand and flicked it on. She didn't want to wake her sisters by turning on the hall light.

After creeping down the hallway and up one flight of stairs, Phoebe reached the attic door. It was open. She glanced around cautiously as she entered the room.

Everything seemed normal.

No strange chill in the air.

No gusting wind.

No eerie light.

No light at all except the beam from her flashlight.

Phoebe crossed to a dusty table where *The Book of Shadows* lay. Piper must have left it there before we went downstairs, Phoebe thought. She gently picked up the book and sat down in an old overstuffed armchair.

There's something to this, she thought, turning a page. There has to be a reason I found this book on this very night. Maybe there's even a reason why I came home when I did—like destiny or something. I'll figure it out, she vowed. And then I'll prove to Prue and Piper that I'm not a flake.

Phoebe turned another page, then stopped short. " 'The Trial of Melinda Warren,' " she said softly.

Melinda Warren! Phoebe was amazed. That was the name of one of her ancestors.

Phoebe remembered Grams going through old photo albums and telling the girls stories about their family. There were no pictures of Melinda Warren, but Grams mentioned her name every time she talked about the family history.

Melinda Warren was the first member of the family to come to America, Phoebe remembered. She emigrated from England to Massachusetts in the 1600s. Grams said that Melinda had suffered some kind of religious persecution.

Could this story be about her? Phoebe wondered. *Our* Melinda Warren? Breathless, Phoebe read on:

> *Melinda Warren left England and arrived in America in 1654 with her two-year-old daughter, Cassandra. Her descendants include branches of the Grants, the Morgans, and the Marstons.*

Phoebe's heart began to race with excitement. Marston! That was her mother's maiden name!

> *Never forgetting her knowledge of witchcraft, Melinda Warren possessed three special powers: The first, telekinesis, or moving objects using only the power of her mind. The second, clairvoyance, or the ability to see the future. Her third power, to stop time.*

Wow, Phoebe thought. Grams never mentioned any of this.

Melinda Warren's powers were discovered when her lover, Hugh Montgomery, betrayed her to the townspeople. She was tried for witchcraft, found guilty, and sentenced to be burned at the stake—a sentence that was never given before.

Phoebe gasped. She couldn't stop reading now.

The townspeople tied her to a stake in the center of the village. The executioner waved a flaming torch before her and asked if she had any last words. This is what she said:

"You may kill me, but you cannot kill my kind. With each generation, the Warren witches will grow stronger and stronger—until, at last, three sisters will arrive. Together, these three sisters will be the most powerful witches the world has ever known. They will be the Charmed Ones."

The executioner then touched his torch to the straw beneath Melinda's feet. She died horribly—but her power lives in every Warren witch's heart. It will be a joyous day when the Charmed Ones are begotten.

Phoebe let the book fall flat on her legs. She tried to take a deep breath, but she couldn't. This was too much to handle.

Three sisters . . . descendants of Melinda Warren . . .

Phoebe remembered the words she chanted earlier that evening. "Bring your powers to we sisters three."

Are we the sisters in the book? Is the book about us? Are we the Charmed Ones?

"No. It can't be." Phoebe held her head in her hands. "It just can't be. That would mean— that would mean we are witches."

Suddenly, a warm breeze blew through the room, and Phoebe noticed the faint scent of burning wood in the air. She sat up straight. What's happening? she wondered.

Phoebe's heart pounded hard in her chest. The pages of *The Book of Shadows* fluttered as the breeze grew fierce.

Her stomach churned as the odor of burning wood grew stronger and stronger. But it wasn't only wood that Phoebe smelled. She gagged when she recognized the scent of burning flesh.

Phoebe wanted to run out of the attic as fast as she could, but it was impossible. She couldn't move. Her feet felt like lead, and her body seemed to be transfixed to the chair. Is something holding me here?

Maybe that spirit board *was* evil. Then Phoebe glanced at *The Book of Shadows*. Maybe this book is evil, too! she thought, panicking.

A bright light flashed out of nowhere, illuminating the attic. Phoebe shielded her eyes with her arms.

The smell of rancid, burning skin was so strong now. Phoebe gagged again.

The light faded. She lowered her arms and gasped at the horrible sight in front of her.

In the center of the room, a charred figure, burned beyond recognition, floated above the floor.

What is it? Phoebe trembled as she stared at its long sooty dress. A woman?

Phoebe whimpered as its gangly, putrid arms opened wide . . . as it floated closer. As its mouth stretched open, exposing black, rotted teeth.

"You called to me," the creature rasped. "You called me for your powers. . . ."

CHAPTER
5

Phoebe struggled to stand up as the charred creature floated closer still. But a force seemed to press her into the chair, keeping her there. She squeezed her eyes shut. "This isn't real. This isn't real. This isn't real," she chanted. "*Please* let this not be real!" she cried.

But when she opened her eyes, the figure hovered right in front of her.

"You called to me," the creature rasped again.

"No!" Phoebe cried. "Go away!"

"You called out for your powers," the ghostly figure told Phoebe. "The sisters three are the most powerful witches the world has ever known. You are the Charmed Ones."

"Who—who are you?" Phoebe stammered.

The woman drifted close to Phoebe, her figure wavering in the strange glow. "I am of you, and you are of me." She stared at Phoebe with her dark, rotting eyes. "I am Melinda Warren."

Phoebe's temples began to pound. Am I really staring at the ghost of Melinda Warren?

"You and your sisters are the Charmed Ones," the spirit repeated. "The sisters three are filled with the power of good, with more power than any other witch. Your magic will be weak at first, but will develop quickly. Remember this: It is most important that the three of you work together. It is the power of three that make you the Charmed Ones. Do you understand?"

Phoebe stared silently at the ghost. This can't be happening, she thought. This can't be real. She closed her eyes again, tightly, to shut out the vision.

"Do you understand?" the ghost demanded. "Answer me!"

Phoebe opened her eyes. "Yes. I—I understand."

"Good. Now, a warning," the spirit said. "The sisters three are powerful, but they are also in great danger. You must be wary."

"Wary of what?" Phoebe whispered.

"Evil warlocks. They will try to steal your powers," the ghost replied. "And the only way to steal a witch's powers . . ." Melinda's ghost paused, baring her rotting teeth in a horrible grimace. " . . . is to kill her."

Phoebe hugged herself. She couldn't stop shaking.

"The warlocks will come," Melinda warned. "I do not know when. But I do know how the first one will strike. He has killed several witches already."

Melinda waved an arm, and a sheet of smoke appeared. An image began to form in the gray cloud.

Phoebe watched carefully. She cringed when the image sharpened and grew clearer.

A tall, hooded man in the shadows of an apartment.

He leans over the body of a pretty blond woman.

An altar glows with candles.

Blood spatters all around it.

The rug, the windows, the walls . . .

The man clutches a knife. Double edged. Jeweled handle.

Stabs at her until she is dead.

"No!" Phoebe's hands covered her mouth as she cried out in horror. She could not watch any longer and quickly looked away.

The image and smoke faded, then disappeared.

Phoebe was shaking harder now. She knew what that horrible image meant: The killer she heard about on the news was killing witches—

and he was going to come after Phoebe and her sisters, and it was all Phoebe's fault.

"I wish I'd never read that incantation!" Phoebe wailed. "I don't want my power! Take it back! Please!"

Melinda frowned. "This is your destiny and the destiny of your sisters! The sisters three can not escape it!" The spirit hovered in the air. "You are the Charmed Ones. You must protect the innocent from the forces of evil."

Phoebe was breathing fast now. "But how?" she cried. "Please, help me! How do we fight a warlock? I don't even know what a warlock is!"

An icy breeze blew through the attic, and Melinda Warren began to slowly fade away.

"Wait!" Phoebe cried. "I don't know what to do! I don't know how to use my power! I don't know anything!"

Melinda grew fainter and fainter. "I can stay no longer," she said.

"But what are we going to do?" Phoebe pleaded.

"*The Book of Shadows* will be your guide," the ghost replied as she faded completely away. "Always remember, The power of three will set you free. . . . The power of three will set you free. . . ."

Phoebe's mind whirled as she tried to take in everything that had happened. She stared down at *The Book of Shadows* in her lap, still open to the page about Melinda Warren.

Could all of this really be true? she wondered. Are we really witches? Could we really be the Charmed Ones?

She glanced at the book again and gasped.

Words began to appear, magically, on the bottom of the page, as though an invisible hand was writing them. Phoebe watched each letter as it formed on the paper:

"The Power of Three Will Set You Free."

"It's true," Phoebe breathed. "It's all true. Everything Melinda said." We're witches, she thought, amazed. Prue, Piper, and I—we're the Charmed Ones.

Phoebe sighed when she thought about what lay ahead of her. Now comes the hard part, she said to herself. How am I going to tell Piper and Prue?

CHAPTER
6

Prue woke the next morning to the sun on her face, streaming in from her bedroom window. To her relief, it was a sparkling, beautiful morning. She was glad the storm was over.

She rolled over onto her side, glanced at the bedside clock, and groaned. Six o'clock, she thought. It's way too early to be up. She closed her eyes, but it was no use. She was awake.

I might as well get an early start at the museum, she thought. She showered and dressed quickly, then grabbed her leather backpack and went to the kitchen to make some coffee. She was surprised to find a very tired-looking Phoebe sitting at the kitchen table with that weird book from the attic.

"Hey, Phoebe," Prue said, dropping the backpack on the table. "You look as if you've been up all night. Are you okay?"

Phoebe glanced up from the book. "I've got to talk to you, Prue. It's important."

Prue hoped that Phoebe wasn't going to bring up Roger again. She didn't want to deal with it right then, or ever, really. "If it's about Roger—"

"Forget about Roger," Phoebe said. "It's worse."

Prue set a kettle of water on the stove to boil and joined Phoebe at the table.

"Are you sick? Are you in some kind of trouble?" she asked.

Phoebe shook her head. "It's nothing like that," she replied. "It's about our powers."

Prue felt all the blood rush to her face. "Powers?" she asked. "You're not still on that, are you?"

Phoebe pointed to *The Book of Shadows*. "It's all in here. It says that after our powers are awakened we—"

"Look, Phoebe." Prue stood up from the table. "I thought you had a problem that you wanted to talk about. But I don't have time to discuss this stupid fantasy of yours." She switched off the stove and grabbed her backpack. "I really hope you get it together soon," she said, and left the kitchen.

She rushed out the front door and slammed

it shut behind her. "Powers," she repeated. Phoebe is getting so weird, Prue thought as she slid into her car. Things are never going to be normal again now that she's here.

Prue started her car and drove to work. She parked near the Museum of Natural History, where she worked as a curator specializing in ancient artifacts.

She strolled around the corner to Dina's, the nearest café. If I ever needed a cup of coffee, Prue thought, I do now.

"A double latte with skim milk, please," Prue ordered. While she waited for her coffee, she couldn't help but worry about Phoebe.

She's going to get herself into trouble quickly, Prue thought, frowning. She hasn't even been home twenty-four hours yet! All that talk about witches—it's just crazy.

Prue's coffee arrived. She grabbed it, paid for it, and spun around to take a lid from the counter. She crashed into the person behind her.

"Whoa!" The guy jumped out of the way as Prue's coffee spilled on the floor.

"I'm so sorry!" Prue cried, without looking at the man. She quickly snatched some napkins from the counter to wipe the coffee off the floor.

The man knelt down to help her. "It's my fault," he told her.

That voice—Prue knew it—Deep, a little

husky, and firm. She glanced at the man's face. Two piercing, intelligent brown eyes met hers.

"Andy?" she asked.

The man smiled. "Prue?"

Prue straightened up slowly. It *was* him. Andy Trudeau, her old high school boyfriend. Prue hadn't seen him in years.

He looks great, Prue thought, eyeing him as he stood up. His rugged face was even more handsome with a few years on it. His wavy, light brown hair was shorter than it used to be, but Prue liked it that way.

"I don't believe it," Andy said. "How are you?"

"Good. How are you?"

"I'm fine." Andy gazed at her for a moment. "I can't believe I'm running into you! What are you doing here?"

Prue smiled to herself. He seemed really glad to see her. She had to admit it was nice seeing him, too. "I'm on my way to work. What are you doing in this part of town?"

"Murder investigation," Andy replied. "Right around the corner. Thought I'd pick up a cup of coffee to help me get through it. Do you have time to sit down for a minute?" He motioned to the coffee mess on the floor. "Let me buy you another cup."

Prue blushed. "Sure," she said, and glanced at her watch. It was still early. She had plenty of time to get to work.

Andy handed her a fresh cup of coffee, and they sat at an empty table by the window.

"So," Prue began, "you're a detective now?"

"Just call me Inspector Trudeau," Andy joked. "Can you believe it? Only in San Francisco would they give detectives such an old-fashioned title."

"I like *Inspector*," Prue said. "It sounds classy."

"I'm liking it better myself." Andy grinned.

"Your dad must be proud," Prue said. Andy came from a long line of police detectives.

"Third generation, you bet he's happy. How about you? Are you taking the world by storm?"

"Not yet," Prue replied. "I'm back living at Grams' house, and, well, things are a little tense at work right now."

Prue paused, thinking of Roger. Her ex-fiancé was also her boss. Ever since she'd broken off their engagement, Roger had been giving her trouble. But Andy doesn't need to know about all that, Prue decided. Just play it cool.

She felt him watching her as she sipped her coffee and her face reddened. "I, uh, heard you moved to Portland," she said. She didn't know what else to say.

"Yes, I'm back." Andy paused. Prue noticed him glancing at the fingers on her left hand. Then he gazed into her eyes. "It sure is good to see you, Prue."

He was checking for a wedding ring, Prue realized. *He's still interested in me.* The wave of happiness that flashed through her at the thought surprised her. *I wouldn't mind rekindling our relationship,* she decided. *I wouldn't mind it at all.*

They had broken up right before high school graduation. Andy had wanted Prue to go to college with him in Oregon, but Prue wanted to go to UCLA. She thought they could have a long-distance relationship. Andy didn't. Case closed.

Prue never forgot him. After all, he was her very first love. And apparently Andy hadn't forgotten her, either. She had been his first love, too.

"You still seeing Roger?" he finally asked.

"How did you know about Roger?" Prue asked, surprised. Andy had been in Portland the whole time she and Roger were together.

"I know people," Andy said, glancing away.

"You checked up on me?" Prue couldn't believe it. She felt indignant, yet flattered at the same time.

"I wouldn't call it that," Andy said.

Prue took a sip of coffee. "Yeah? What would you call it then?"

"Inquiring minds want to know?" Andy smiled sheepishly.

Prue laughed. "You checked up on me."

"Hey, what can I say? I'm a detective." He

nervously swished a coffee stirrer in his cup. "So? You still with him?"

Prue shook her head. "No. We broke up a while ago."

Andy opened his mouth as if he was about to say something, then he closed it.

"What?" Prue asked playfully.

"It's just so strange that I ran into you today," Andy replied.

"Why?" Prue encouraged him.

"Because I've been thinking about you a lot lately," he said, lowering his eyes. "I mean, more than usual." He raised his head and gazed at Prue.

He's quieter than he used to be, Prue thought. More serious. She liked that. She liked that a lot.

"I was really sorry when I heard Grams died," Andy said. "She was a wonderful woman. I used to love hanging out with you at your Grams' house."

Prue smiled at him. It was nice to be with someone who remembered. Roger never seemed interested in her past at all. He hadn't even liked Grams that much. He'd thought she was too kooky. But Andy—

A whirlwind of emotions caught Prue by surprise. Be careful, she warned herself. Don't get carried away. After her breakup with Roger, she promised to give herself time to recuperate. She didn't want to jump right into another relationship. But it *has* been almost a year, she thought.

Prue glanced at her watch. Oops. Ten to nine. She hadn't realized how long they'd been talking.

"I guess it's time," she told him. "I'd better be getting to work."

"Yeah. Me, too."

They rose from the table and left the café. They lingered outside the door for a second, awkwardly.

Prue had the feeling Andy did not want to say good-bye. "Um, so is it the same phone number at the old house?" he asked her.

Prue tried to stifle a smile. She found a pen and a piece of paper in her backpack and scribbled her telephone number for him. Giving Andy my number isn't exactly jumping into a relationship, she decided. "Here you go," she said, handing it to him.

"I'll call you soon," Andy replied, tucking the paper into his jacket.

"Great!" Prue pecked him on the cheek and hurried around the corner to the museum. She felt a flutter of excitement as she thought of Andy. I guess I never realized how much I missed him, she thought.

"Perfect," Piper said as she snipped a bit of rosemary from a bush in the garden on the side of Halliwell manor. She cut a few pieces of fresh basil as well. She needed them for the recipe that she would be cooking when she auditioned at Quake that afternoon.

Herbs in hand, Piper rounded the corner of the house and started up the front steps. To her surprise, Phoebe was sitting at the top of the stairs in her bike shorts, nursing a cup of coffee. The newspaper was open on her lap.

She looks tired, Piper thought. She smiled at Phoebe, hoping to cheer her up. "You're up early," Piper said.

"I never went to sleep," Phoebe replied.

"So what were you doing all night?" Piper asked.

"Reading. I was reading *The Book of Shadows.*" She hesitated. "According to the book, one of our ancestors was—" She gave Piper a sideways glance. "She was a witch. Her name was Melinda Warren."

Piper rolled her eyes. Even *she* didn't believe in witches. She leaned in close to Phoebe and whispered, "And we have a cousin who's a drunk, an aunt who's manic, and a father who's invisible."

"I'm serious," Phoebe insisted. "Melinda Warren possessed powers. *Three* powers. She could move objects with her mind, she could see the future, and she could stop time. Before she was burned at the stake, she vowed that each generation of Warren witches would become stronger and stronger—culminating in the arrival of three sisters."

Piper raised an eyebrow. "Three sisters?" she repeated.

"These sisters would be the most powerful witches the world has ever known. They're good witches, and . . ."

"Let me guess. They would be us, right? Oh, Phoebe, this is nuts."

"Piper, there's more," Phoebe went on. She tapped the newspaper. "I was just reading about the latest woman who was murdered by that psycho. She had the same tattoo as all the other victims. And that tattoo is the same as the design on the cover of *The Book of Shadows!*"

She pointed to a photograph in the newspaper. It showed the tattoo on the chest of the latest victim: three arcs intersecting inside a circle. "See?"

Piper stared at the photo. Phoebe was right. It was the same symbol. A tiny shiver trickled through her body, but she shrugged it off. "So what? Maybe it's some old Celtic symbol. Lots of people probably have tattoos like that. It could just be some new trend."

"Piper, those women were witches," Phoebe said. "I'm sure of it." She stared at the newspaper again. "Maybe they had powers—and something evil was after them to get those powers, powers like Melinda Warren had. Powers like *we* have."

Piper gritted her teeth. *Maybe Prue is right. Maybe Phoebe is playing some kind of stupid joke on us, trying to see how much we'll believe.* "Stop kidding around, Phoebe. It's not funny anymore."

Phoebe dropped the paper. She stared into Piper's eyes. "Look at me, Piper," she said. "Do I really look like I'm kidding around?"

Piper gazed back at her sister. Phoebe didn't seem to be joking. That was the problem. "Phoebe, how could we be witches?" she asked gently. "We don't have powers. Not that I know of, anyway."

"He's going to come after us next," Phoebe warned. "We have to be prepared."

Piper felt another little shiver, stronger this time. She started to think about the killer out there. *But no,* she told herself. *I've got a big audition this afternoon. I've got to concentrate. We are* not *witches.*

Still clutching the herbs, Piper sat down beside her sister. "Phoebe, listen. We're not witches, okay? Maybe Prue is sometimes something that rhymes with witch, but we're not actual witches. We don't have any special powers. And besides, Grams wasn't a witch, and as far as we know, neither was Mom."

Phoebe opened her mouth to protest. Piper clapped a hand over it.

"Let me finish," Piper said. "Second, we don't have tattoos of that weird symbol, and we're not about to get any." She at glanced at her sister. "*Right*, Phoebe?"

Phoebe nodded, her mouth still covered by Piper's hand.

"So no one is coming after us," Piper finished. She removed her hand from Phoebe's mouth.

Phoebe licked her lips. "Prue didn't believe me either," she replied, shaking her head.

"Where is Prue, anyway?" Piper asked.

"She left for work early." Phoebe turned her glance to the street as a car pulled up in front of the house—a shiny, red Mustang convertible.

"Wow," Phoebe breathed. "Some car."

"That's Jeremy," Piper said. "You get to meet him at last!" She grinned as she watched her boyfriend saunter up the front walk in a light blue button-down shirt and khakis that hung off his hips just right.

He's so gorgeous, she thought—tall, lean, handsome. Piper felt another little shiver run down her back, this time of happiness.

At the foot of the stairs, Jeremy bowed. "Chef Halliwell," he said, kissing Piper's hand.

Piper giggled. "Jeremy, this is my little sister, Phoebe."

Jeremy took Phoebe's hand and kissed it, too. "It's wonderful to meet another beautiful Halliwell sister," he said.

"Wow. He can sure lay it on thick," Phoebe said with a grin. "Just like you said, Piper."

Piper elbowed Phoebe in the ribs. "What are you doing here so early, Jeremy?" she asked.

"Well, since today is your big audition, I thought I'd take you to breakfast. I'll drop you off at the restaurant afterward. Then I figured we could go out later—to celebrate your new job."

Piper hopped to her feet and kissed him. "You're so sweet," she said. "I'll just grab my things. I'll be right back."

Piper dashed inside the house. She grabbed her chef's outfit and her grocery bags full of ingredients. When she returned to the front porch, she found Phoebe and Jeremy chatting about the weather.

"I'm ready," Piper said. She started down the stairs and turned to Phoebe. "Have a good day today," she told her. "Or try to, at least."

Phoebe grabbed her by the arm. "Piper, wait," she whispered. "I've got to talk to you. We're in real danger! We need to develop our powers—"

"Come on, Phoebe, give it a rest," Piper interrupted. "We don't have any special powers, okay?"

Jeremy took Piper by the shoulders and stared into her eyes. "But you do have a special power," he told her. "I'm sure of it."

"Huh?" Piper said. "What are you talking about?"

"Over me." Jeremy grinned his sexy, lop-sided grin.

Piper kissed him again. It was a stupid joke, but she didn't mind.

Jeremy grabbed the groceries, and they started for the car.

"Good luck today," Phoebe called, her voice kind of flat.

Piper waved to her sister as Phoebe stood and started into the house.

Jeremy held the passenger door open for her and placed the groceries in the back. Then he got into the driver's seat and started the car.

"What was that all about?" he asked. "That stuff about special powers?"

Piper shook her head in exasperation. She didn't know what she was going to do about Phoebe. She just hoped that Phoebe didn't stay on this witch kick too long. "Jeremy," she said, "you wouldn't believe me if I told you."

CHAPTER 7

Prue sat at her desk, doodling on a notepad, daydreaming. She couldn't stop thinking about seeing Andy that morning. It's as if he showed up just in time, she thought, just when I needed a lift. Like magic.

She quickly tossed the idea of magic out of her mind. Now you're thinking like Phoebe, she scolded herself.

Still, Prue hadn't gone on a single date since she broke up with Roger. Plenty of guys had asked her out, but she was never interested. She told herself she needed time to get over Roger, time to learn to trust someone again.

She'd begun to think that would never happen. She was afraid she'd never trust any man enough to love him.

I probably shouldn't trust Andy either, she thought. Why should he be different from the others? After all, he was the one who broke off our relationship. He couldn't handle the distance. Maybe that was an excuse. Maybe we were just getting too serious, and it made him nervous.

Even so, Prue couldn't help remembering their time together. How they would sit in each other's arms and talk for hours. It had been so comfortable.

A knock on her office door startled Prue back to her senses. She glanced up to see Roger standing in the doorway.

Prue had to admit Roger was good looking, but she wasn't attracted to him at all anymore. Only thirty, Roger had risen rapidly through the museum world. He was tall, blond, and elegantly dressed in his designer suit. Still, Prue had always thought he wore his pants too high on his waist. Gold wire-rimmed glasses were perched on his nose. The frame was straight and nicely shaped but, Prue thought as he approached her desk, had a sort of snippy look to it.

"How's the Beals Collection going, Prue?" Roger asked. "Anything new to report?"

"Yes. The artifacts should be arriving around two o'clock," she replied. "I'll supervise the unpacking this afternoon and take the inventory to make sure it's all there and in good shape."

"Good. Why don't you take a long lunch today?" Roger suggested. "I know you've been working really hard. You deserve it."

"Thanks, Roger," Prue replied. "I'm glad to see that you've noticed." Finally, Prue added to herself.

Roger hesitated. "Fine. Well, I'm on my way to a board meeting now," he said.

Prue rose to her feet. She usually accompanied Roger to the meetings with the board. "I'll just get my purse," she said.

Roger held out his hand to stop her. "That won't be necessary," he said. "I'm meeting with the board alone today."

"Why?" Prue asked, surprised. "I always go with you."

"Uh . . . it was at their request." Roger smiled uncomfortably, as if he were hiding something. "I don't know why. Perhaps they're going to reprimand me for some small infraction."

Prue sat down, eyeing him suspiciously. Reprimand him? Roger was so full of himself he'd never suspect anyone of thinking he'd done a bad job.

"I just wanted to let you know I won't be back in the office until this afternoon," he said. "I'll brief you about the meeting around three o'clock, okay?"

He grinned and flicked his Mont Blanc pen at her.

Prue had given it to him as a gift after he'd

received his master's degree. Roger liked the fact that it was expensive. He took every opportunity he could to wave the pen around, from signing credit-card receipts to gesturing with it to make a point. It was his status symbol—one of them, anyway—and it really annoyed Prue. She wished that she had never bought the stupid thing.

"All right, Roger," Prue replied. "See you later."

Roger nodded and strutted down the hall, whistling.

He's up to something, Prue thought. He's never gone to a board meeting without me before. If the board was going to criticize him, she wished she could be there to witness it. She'd love to see him get knocked off his high horse.

But Prue was sure that wasn't the reason he was going alone. Roger would never admit that anyone thought he was anything but perfect—that's why she thought his excuse sounded so phony.

She picked up her ordinary ball-point pen and drew swirls on her notepad. What could she do? Roger was her boss. She couldn't force him to take her to the meeting.

At least she had the Beals Collection to work on. It was her pet project, and it was going beautifully. She had discovered a trove of ancient Asian artifacts that had never been exhibited publicly before. The museum would make history with this exhibit. Once the board sees how well it turns out, Prue thought, I'm sure I'll be promoted.

Maybe I'll even get to be Roger's boss, she thought wickedly. That would be fun.

With a cup of coffee in hand, Prue strode through the grand-stone entrance of the museum, across the marble lobby, and into the offices. She had just finished eating lunch and was bracing herself for a long afternoon of cataloging.

Just outside Prue's office, museum workers were unpacking large wooden crates filled with ancient Asian artifacts. Roger stood nearby with a clipboard, checking the inventory.

What's he doing? Prue wondered, glancing at an antique vase on the carpet. These artifacts are part of my project. *I'm* supposed to oversee the inventory. Roger knows that.

"What's going on?" Prue asked.

Roger nodded and pointed his Mont Blanc at Prue. "There's been a change of plans regarding the Beals exhibition."

If he points that pen at me one more time . . . Prue thought irritably.

"The extra money you helped raise through those private donations has sparked a lot of corporate interest in the show," he told her. "The Beals artifacts will now become part of our permanent collection."

"That's wonderful!" Prue let out a breath of relief. For a moment she'd thought something had gone wrong with the project.

"Which is why the board wants someone a little more . . . *qualified* to handle the collection from now on," Roger continued, waving his pen.

What? Prue raised an eyebrow. She was an expert on the Beals artifacts. She'd worked her butt off for months on the exhibition.

"You look surprised," Roger said.

"Surprised?" Prue snapped, trying to control her tone. "I'm furious! I tracked down these artifacts, convinced the Beals family to lend them to us, and raised the money to finance the exhibition! This show wouldn't have happened without me!"

Roger glanced at the floor as he nervously slid his pen into his shirt pocket.

So that's why he didn't want me at the board meeting this morning, Prue fumed. He realized this was a great project and convinced the board to let him run it. He stole the project from me!

"*You're* the person 'a little more qualified,' aren't you, Roger?" she accused.

Roger straightened his posture, trying to intimidate her. "I could hardly say no to the board of directors, could I?" he asked. "But I know you'll be happy for me. After all, what's good for me is definitely good for you."

Prue glared at the pen in his shirt pocket as he spoke. To her it symbolized Roger's smugness, his insincerity, and all the underhanded things he'd done to her. Right now she really hated that pen.

"Right, Miss Halliwell?" Roger added.

"*Miss Halliwell?*" Prue asked. "Since when did we stop being on a first name basis? Since you decided to take credit for my work? Or since I returned your engagement ring, *Roger?*"

Roger smirked. "Take your pick. When are you going to realize the quality of your work doesn't matter? You know why the president *really* hired you?"

"Why?" Prue asked.

"You were wearing a tight little dress on your interview, and he thought you'd make nice eye candy." Roger laughed. "He was right!"

Prue narrowed her eyes. A surge of anger welled up inside of her. She couldn't believe what he'd just said to her. She realized months ago that he wasn't the person she'd thought he was, but she'd had no idea he was such a slimy little rat!

She turned away from him and stepped toward her office.

"Prue—wait," Roger said.

Prue whirled around. "What?"

"I feel I should say something—if only to avoid a lawsuit," he joked.

Prue didn't think the comment was funny. She stood outside her office door, glaring at him, her anger building. Then she noticed a spot on the pocket of his expensive white shirt. A dark blue spot, spreading quickly over the cloth. Ink! From his precious pen. Prue grinned.

Roger noticed her stare and glanced down. "Oh, no!" he cried. He yanked the pen out of his pocket and squinted at it, trying to find the leak—it broke in two, squirting ink all over Roger's face.

Roger cried out in horror, sputtering ink out of his mouth. His face, his hair, his clothes— everything was covered in dark blue ink.

Prue burst out laughing.

Roger glared at her, then hurried down the hall toward his office.

Prue stepped into her own office and shut the door behind her. "Deep breaths," she told herself, trying to calm down. She sat behind her desk. "Relax and think."

She couldn't believe what Roger was doing. Taking credit for her project, and taking it away from her! When it had all been *her* idea!

If that's the way he works, it's no wonder he's risen so quickly, she fumed. Well, I won't let him get away with it. I'm going to fight for this project. I deserve to be in charge of the Beals Collection. It's time I take the credit for once!

Prue sat still in her chair for a few minutes,

steeling herself for the confrontation ahead. Then she grabbed her purse and marched out of her office and down the hall.

She charged past Roger's secretary's desk and into his office. She was glad his assistant was out sick that day.

Roger sat at his desk, facing the window, talking on the phone. He'd already changed his shirt and was knotting the tie around his neck.

Of course he would keep extra shirts and ties in his office, Prue thought. That's just like him. Always worried about how he looks.

Roger was too busy talking to hear her come in. "Well, it *was* my idea to spark corporate interest through private donations," Prue heard him say.

He must be talking to someone on the museum board, Prue realized. And that wasn't his idea—it was mine!

"Besides," Roger was saying, "not only have I been with this project since its inception, we both know who *really* secured the entire exhibit."

Roger swiveled in his leather chair to face his desk—and Prue.

Prue put her hands on her hips, staring daggers at him. Roger's expression changed from smug self-satisfaction to awkward surprise.

"P-P-Prue—" he stammered.

That's it, Prue thought. I refuse to work for someone who treats me this way. "I quit," she announced.

Roger spoke quietly into the phone. "I'm going to have to call you back." He hung up the phone. "Think about this, Prue."

"Lousy job, lousy pay, lousy boss," Prue said. "What's to think about?"

"Your future," Roger replied. "Because, believe me, if you leave without notice, you can kiss any references—"

"Don't threaten me, Roger," Prue told him. Her mouth tightened into a thin line.

Roger shrugged. "You know me. I had to try." He stood up, moving toward her, and sat on the edge of his desk. "Listen," he said, softening his voice. "You're hurt. You're angry. Your pride is wounded. I understand all that. It's clouded your perception. You can't see that I'm doing you a favor."

"A *favor*? Do you think I'm that stupid?" she demanded.

"I *had* to take the exhibit away from you," Roger insisted. "If I hadn't, the board would have brought in a total stranger in my place to oversee it." He leaned in closer to her, smiling gently. "Think about it, Prue. *I'm* here for you, not some stranger. You should be thanking me, not leaving me."

Thanking him! Prue thought. He'll say anything to get out of a tight spot. She could not believe that she ever considered marrying such a sneaky, lying, selfish weasel.

Roger studied her face, his smile slowly fading.

"Don't worry, Roger. You don't need me," Prue said. "I'm certain that your razor-sharp intellect will make quick work of the seventy-five computer disks and thousands of pages of research I've left in my office."

Let's see him actually *do* something for a change, she thought.

Roger aimed a finger at Prue. "You're going to regret this," he told her.

"Oh, I don't think so," Prue shot back. "I thought breaking up with you was the best thing I'd ever done. But this definitely tops that."

Roger's face fell. He stared at her with his mouth open.

"Good-bye, Roger," she said in a light-hearted voice, then turned on her heel, and sauntered out of his office with a smile.

"I hope there are no office supplies in your purse!" he called after her.

Prue stopped in her tracks. He couldn't just let it go, could he? He always has to have the last word. I could wring his neck! She wrapped her hands around an imaginary neck and pretended to strangle it as she marched into the hall.

"Help!" Roger cried out from his office.

Now what is he up to? Prue wondered.

"Somebody, help!" Roger screamed louder.

Prue turned, peered into Roger's office, and gasped.

He lay on the floor in front of his desk, tugging at his necktie, gasping for breath. His face was swollen and red, bulging over the tie, which had jammed around his neck like a noose.

"H-h-h-g-g-g—" Roger croaked.

Oh my God, Prue thought. He's choking!

CHAPTER 8

Prue—help me!" Roger gagged.

Prue stared at him in shock as he struggled to yank his necktie off. The tie seemed to be strangling him—all by itself!

She rushed to his side and knelt down, trying to unknot the tie. It was so tight around Roger's neck she couldn't loosen it.

"It won't come off!" she cried. As she held the tie, it seemed to tighten even more, pressing firmly against Roger's Adam's apple.

Roger's eyes watered as he clutched his throat, desperate for air.

She yanked on the tie again, but nothing would loosen it. The more she struggled with it, the tighter it became.

What's going on?

How could this be happening?

"Prue—" Roger gasped, touching her arm. His eyes were nearly bulging out of his head.

He can't breathe. He's dying! Prue realized, horrified. "Hold on, Roger," she cried.

She hurried to his desk, opened a drawer, and snatched up a pair of scissors. She returned to Roger's side. His face had turned deep purple. Prue quickly lifted his head and shoulders from the floor as he struggled to breathe.

She pulled the tie taut and snipped it loose with the scissors. Roger's head dropped to the floor with a thud.

"Oh, Prue," he said in a raspy whisper. "Thank you." He gave her a tiny smile.

"Are you okay?" she asked.

"Yes," he said, his smile widening. "You came back. I knew you still wanted me."

Prue let the scissors fall to the floor—right next to Roger's head. What a loser, she thought angrily. He probably faked this whole scene just to get back at me for quitting!

"You're a jerk," Prue spat out as she stood up to leave. "I don't want you. And I still quit."

Piper's white chef's hat drooped into her face as she spooned sauce over a roast of pork. She pushed the hat away.

Sunlight streamed into Quake's shiny stainless steel kitchen, reflecting off the gleaming pots and pans hanging above the stove. Even

Piper's white kitchen jacket glowed in the afternoon light.

She worked quickly and carefully, concentrating on every detail. Chef Moore had given her exactly one hour to prepare her audition meal, and the hour was nearly up.

Everything's going well so far, she thought. She spooned some red sauce from a pot and tasted it. "Mmmm." The sauce for the pasta was almost ready. Now was the perfect time to add the port wine.

She opened the bottle of wine that Jeremy had given her—the final touch for her pasta recipe. She sniffed the bottle. Delicious! This would transform her pasta sauce from ordinary to fabulous!

Piper carefully measured out a quarter cup of port. She was just about to add it to the pasta sauce when Sheridan Moore breezed in.

"Your time is up!" he announced in his French accent, clapping his hands.

Sheridan Moore was the head chef at Quake. Wiry and dark haired, he was fairly young to be such an important chef. Piper found his European manners a little intimidating, but he was a remarkable cook, and she really wanted to work in his kitchen.

"I am ready to taste your meal," he told her.

No! Not yet! Piper thought, clutching the measuring cup of port wine. She hadn't had time to add it to the pasta sauce, and without it, the sauce wouldn't taste right. What was she going to do?

"Chef Moore," Piper said. "Um . . . I—"

The chef ignored her, glancing at an index card. "Let us see," he said. "Roast pork with gratin of fennel and penne with a port giblet sauce."

Piper wanted desperately to add the port to the sauce, but Chef Moore stood between her and the pasta dish, blocking her way.

"Chef Moore, I—" Piper began.

Before she had a chance to finish, the chef picked up a fork and hovered over the pasta.

"I have to tell you something," Piper said.

He paused, spearing a few pieces of pasta with the fork. "What is it?"

"The port—" she said.

He nodded. "Ah yes, the port. Without it, the sauce is nothing more than a salty marinara. A recipe from a woman's magazine. Puh!"

"I didn't have time to—" Piper tried again.

"Ah-ah!" The chef cut her off with a wave of his hand. With his other hand, he dipped the pasta into the sauce and raised the fork to his lips, preparing to taste the unfinished dish.

Piper was frantic. "But, but—" I can't let him eat it, she thought. She'd never get the job if he tasted that sauce. "No! Wait!" she cried, waving her hands. "Don't eat it. Stop! Stop!"

Chef Moore stopped. He stood as still as a statue, the fork hovering near his open mouth.

"Thank you so much," Piper said. "I just need two seconds . . ." She stared at the chef, who still stood frozen in place, the fork at his lips.

No one told me he had a sense of humor, Piper thought, laughing nervously.

"Chef Moore?" Piper asked. She tapped his shoulder. He didn't move an inch. What was he doing? She waved a hand in front of his face. "Chef Moore?"

He didn't respond. His eyes didn't even blink.

"Hello?" Piper waved her hand once again. *"Hel-lo!"* she said a little louder.

Piper glanced at the stove—at the pot of boiling water that had frozen mid-bubble.

"What is going on?" Piper murmured, her heart thudding heavily against her chest. She glanced at the clock hanging on the wall. The second hand isn't moving either, she realized. She rested her ear against the refrigerator. It's not humming! Everything has stopped dead, Piper thought. Everything except me!

She stared at the motionless Chef Moore in horror. Did I do that to him? she asked herself. Is Phoebe right? Am I . . . am I really a witch?

CHAPTER 9

I–i've frozen time," Piper murmured. "At least, I think I have." She stared at the unmoving chef in front of her, ready to taste her pasta dish.

Without thinking, she snatched up a baster and filled it with some port. She dribbled the wine onto the pasta and dabbed a few drops onto Chef Moore's forkful.

Chef Moore suddenly blinked and popped the pasta into his mouth.

Wow! Piper thought. I can't believe this is happening. She glanced at the water on the stove. It was bubbling again. The clock was ticking and the refrigerator was humming. Everything was back to normal.

She looked at Chef Moore.

"*C'est magnifique!*" he declared as he swallowed the pasta. "This is fabulous!" He shook Piper's hand. "Welcome aboard—you get the job. What do you say? Can you start this evening?"

Piper beamed. She'd done it! "Of course," she replied. "Tonight is fine."

"Good. See you at five." Chef Moore took another forkful of Piper's pasta and sauntered out of the kitchen.

Piper slowly pulled off her hat. Her hands were shaking.

She was thrilled to get the job, but what had just happened? Had she really frozen time? How did she do it?

Phoebe, Piper thought. She must know something about this.

I've got to call her—now!

Phoebe was halfway out the front door when the phone rang. She glanced back at it, irritated.

The machine will pick it up, she decided. I've got other things to worry about.

She ran down the front steps and unlocked her bike. Then she pedaled off to Haight Ashbury, a funky neighborhood where she knew she'd find at least one book shop specializing in Wicca and witchcraft.

She couldn't get the vision of Melinda Warren out of her mind. "Evil warlocks want to steal your powers," Melinda had said. "The warlocks will come. . . ."

But Melinda hadn't told her much else. She hadn't said how a witch could fight a warlock. How do I even recognize one? Phoebe wondered anxiously. Do I have to wait until he's about to stab me with a knife?

She rode through the hilly city, barely noticing how it sparkled in the sunlight. Once in the Haight, she stopped in front of a shop called Enchanted.

It's either a Wicca store or a lingerie shop, Phoebe decided. But the long velvet capes covering the store window made her think that it was probably a magic shop.

Phoebe locked her bike to a parking meter and went inside the store.

The scent of patchouli incense engulfed her as soon as she entered the dark shop. A neon sign buzzed over a doorway advertising tarot-card readings given in the back room. A young woman wearing a long, tight black dress and black nail polish leaned on a glass countertop, which held small gold pots and odd-looking utensils. Behind her, the wall was lined with glass jars containing a variety of herbs.

The woman smiled at Phoebe. "Blessed be," she said.

"Huh?" Phoebe responded.

"I'm wishing you well," the woman said. She eyed Phoebe up and down. "You're new to Wicca, aren't you? Feel free to ask any questions."

"Uh, yeah. Thanks," Phoebe replied, but inside she was thinking, uh, yeah, *right*. She glanced at a bearded man with a dirty T-shirt three sizes too small for him checking out a table of knives. Like I would ever want to call attention to myself in a place like this. She could just hear it now. Yes, excuse me. Um, exactly what is a warlock and how would I go about killing one? Phoebe shook her head. I don't think so. I'm better off finding the answer to that question on my own.

She wandered through the narrow aisles of the store—love spells, fertility candles, wind chimes, postcards that read, "All my friends call me a witch."

"Blessed be," Phoebe muttered. She picked up a *Wicca for Dummies* book. "This place is a total tourist trap."

Phoebe had just about given up hope when she turned the corner into the last aisle. There, in the back of the shop, was a small section of books on witches and warlocks.

She scanned the titles and chose the thickest book, called *Witches and Warlocks—the Eternal Battle*. Phoebe crouched in the aisle, paging through the heavy book until she found something interesting:

> *The conflict between the sects originated at the dawn of time and is bound by the inherent differences between witches and warlocks.*

Oddly enough, warlocks were originally witches, making their inferiority complexes understandable. They are the bad seeds of the Wicca world.

As "witches gone bad," warlocks are determined to make their mark by torturing innocents. Another quest is to kill witches and steal their powers. Warlocks have also been known to form agreements with demons to further their goals.

All of this is done in an effort to strengthen their own power to perform evil deeds.

Phoebe's heart raced as she looked away from the book. After her experience the night before, she knew she had to believe what she had just read. All of this stuff has been going on in some kind of underworld for centuries, she realized. And regular, everyday people are totally clueless about it!

Phoebe read on:

Warlocks have been growing stronger and stronger with each generation.

Okay, okay, she thought. But how do I know one when I see one? She scanned the book further:

Warlocks usually appear in human form. However, they can easily take on a monstrous

*demeanor. Unfortunately, it is difficult to rec-
ognize warlocks until they have revealed their
evil powers.*

Just my luck, Phoebe thought, slapping the
book shut. She carried it to the cash register.
Yesterday, I never would have believed any of
this stuff. Now, I'll never be able to trust a
stranger again. Or even a friend, she thought
with horror.

Anyone could be a warlock. *Anyone.*

She stared at the back of a man standing in
line in front of her, buying a box of candles.

For all I know, he could be a warlock, Phoebe
thought nervously. Or *he* could, she mused,
glancing at a pimply teenage boy who strolled
out of the back room, picking his nose.

Or he could, she thought as a tall, handsome,
square-jawed man entered the shop. Then a
shock of recognition rattled her.

That's Andy Trudeau! she realized. Prue's
old boyfriend!

Phoebe left the checkout line as casually as
she could. She shoved the heavy book back
on the shelf and ducked behind a tall rack of
velvet capes as Andy browsed through the
store.

What in the world is *he* doing here? Phoebe
thought. Isn't he a cop or something?

She didn't want Andy to see her, and she
didn't want to talk to him. It wasn't against the

law to be in a Wicca shop, but Phoebe was sure that Andy would ask questions.

Besides, Phoebe had had enough trouble lately with Prue and her boyfriends.

Andy made a move toward the books. Phoebe crossed to another aisle and slipped behind a display of ceremonial knives.

Too late. Andy spotted her and smiled.

Oh no, she thought. Here he comes.

"Phoebe Halliwell?" he asked. "It *is* you. It's so weird that I should run into you."

Phoebe plastered a fake nice-to-see-you smile on her face. "Andy! Hi. Wow, I haven't seen you in a long time."

"I know. So what are you doing here? I didn't know you were into Wicca."

Phoebe didn't meet his eyes. "Oh, me? No, I'm not into this stuff at all. But, um, I thought I might get an astrology book, you know—I like to read my horoscope sometimes." She paused, this time looking him straight in the face. "So, what about you? What are you doing here?"

"I'm on a case," he answered. "Investigating a string of murders."

"Murders? Was someone killed in this store?" Phoebe asked, feigning innocence.

Andy stared into her eyes so intensely that Phoebe felt a little bit uncomfortable.

"No," he replied. "Six witches have been killed. Maybe you've heard about it?"

Phoebe shifted her weight, withering under

the strength of his stare. "Sure, of course," she said. "I think I saw something on the news."

He kept staring into her eyes, unwavering. What's with him? Phoebe wondered. He was making her very nervous now. He can't think that I'm a witch—can he?

"Come on, Phoebe. What are you *really* doing here?" he asked firmly. "You never could hide your secrets very well."

"I told you, I—"

"No," he interrupted. "Tell me the truth. You're not practicing Wicca, are you?"

Phoebe glanced at Andy suspiciously, but she didn't want to answer him. Especially after reading that book about warlocks. What if he was a warlock? Wouldn't he kill her if he found out she was a witch?

"I'm warning you," Andy continued. "For your sake." His eyes cut into her. "Being a witch—it's not very safe these days."

Phoebe bit her bottom lip to keep it from trembling. Andy *cannot* know that I'm a witch, she reminded herself. He can't possibly. She avoided his eyes again, but she could still feel his stare burning into her.

"I was just in the neighborhood, you know," Phoebe said as brightly as she could. "Browsing, killing time . . ."

Andy nodded, but she had a sense that he didn't believe her.

He turned his attention to the table in front

of them. Two rows of ceremonial knives lay on a bed of red velvet.

Andy reached for a gold knife with a jeweled handle. He held it up to the light.

"This is it," he said softly, gazing at the knife, then at Phoebe, then back to the knife again.

"What—what are you talking about?" Phoebe stammered. She looked at the knife and gasped. It was the same kind of knife Melinda had warned her about. Phoebe remembered the smoky image her ancestor had shown her in the attic and shuddered. It's the same kind of knife the warlock used to kill those other witches. The same kind of knife he would use to try to kill Phoebe and her sisters if he knew about them!

"This knife," Andy explained, still staring at it. "The murderer likes to use a double-sided knife exactly like this one."

The blade flashed in the light. Phoebe shuddered again. Not just because of the way Andy was holding the knife. It was the creepy way Andy was suddenly talking. He spoke in a slow monotone, almost as if he was in a trance.

"The murderer stalks his victim for weeks, sometimes months," Andy murmured. "He waits for the right moment, when she's feeling safe, or when she's performing a Wiccan ritual. Then he sneaks up behind her. . . ."

Phoebe stared at Andy. His eyes stayed on the knife. He doesn't even seem to be talking to

me, she thought. It's as if he's lost in another
world.

"The murderer raises his knife over the victim," Andy breathed. "Like this."

Andy slowly lifted the knife, both hands
grasping the jeweled handle.

"Andy—what are you doing?" Phoebe nervously asked.

He didn't answer. His eyes glittered
strangely.

Phoebe glanced around the shop. It seemed
to have cleared out. Even the woman behind
the counter was gone. Where is everybody? she
wondered.

She focused her eyes on Andy's hands. They
gripped the knife so hard his knuckles turned
white.

"Andy—" she said again.

But Andy wasn't listening. He raised the
jeweled knife over his head.

Oh my God. He's going to kill me, Phoebe
realized in a panic. He's going to kill me right
here in the store!

CHAPTER

10

No, Andy! Please," Phoebe screamed. "Please don't kill me!"

A tiny bell chimed as the door to the shop quickly opened. The woman wearing the long black dress burst into the store.

Startled, Andy dropped the knife. It fell to the wooden floor with a thud.

Phoebe released her breath. She was so scared, she hadn't even realized that she was holding it.

"What's going on in here?" the woman in black cried. "What's wrong? Who screamed?"

Andy stared at Phoebe, his mouth open in surprise. "Everything's fine," he quickly assured the woman. "My friend here just had a little shock, that's all."

"Oh. Okay." The woman glanced at her watch. "I guess my break is over," she said, and took her place behind the long glass counter.

Andy turned to Phoebe. "Are you okay?" he asked her.

Phoebe glanced down at the knife, where it lay, harmless now, on the wooden floor. She was still too shaken and confused to reply. What just happened here? she wondered.

"Phoebe, I'm so sorry." Andy gently touched her shoulder. "I didn't mean to scare you. It's just this murder case—Well, sometimes I get a little carried away."

A little? Phoebe found herself gasping for breath. She couldn't help taking a step away from Andy. I can't trust anybody now, she remembered.

"This investigation has been so weird," Andy continued. "And mysterious. So I've been trying to get inside the murderer's head, trying to figure out what and when his next move might be. Whoever he is, this guy is really good."

Phoebe nodded, still shaken. Of course, she thought, that's how he works. He's got to think like the murderer.

Still, she thought, it's kind of strange to run into him today, after all these years. Is it a coincidence that I just happened to run into Andy so soon after I read the incantation from *The Book of Shadows*? The day after

Melinda Warren warned me that a man was going to try to kill me and my sisters with a jewel-encrusted, double-sided knife? She cast Andy a nervous glance as she backed away from him.

Andy crouched down to pick up the knife, then placed it on top of the velvet tablecloth.

The woman behind the counter shot him a dirty look. "Be careful with that," she said to Andy. "Those knives are expensive."

"Sorry," he apologized. "I was just looking."

Phoebe tried to calm herself. Andy is a detective, she reasoned. Of course he would know what kind of weapon the killer uses. And if all the victims were witches, of course he would have to look into Wicca and things like that.

"So—isn't this funny?" Andy asked, his trance-like manner gone now.

"Isn't *what* funny?" Phoebe asked.

"Didn't Prue tell you?" he asked.

Phoebe was confused. "Tell me what?"

Andy slapped his hand to his forehead. "Of course she didn't tell you. How could she? I ran into her this morning near the museum," he explained. "And now I bump into you. Isn't that weird?"

Phoebe's breath caught in her throat. "That *is* weird," she said. And she meant it.

"Yeah," Andy said. "It was really great to see Prue again."

Andy smiled at Phoebe, but instead of making her feel warm, it turned her blood ice cold.

"I have a feeling you're going to see a lot more of me around Halliwell Manor," he added.

"The chosen ones? The Charmed Ones?" Prue sat next to Phoebe at the bar of Quake later that evening. She stared at her youngest sister in disbelief. "Phoebe, I told you this morning. That witch stuff is insane."

Prue gave a slight smile to the bartender as he served her a clear mug filled with coffee. He set a shot of tequila in front of Phoebe and wandered away.

The two sisters had come to give Piper moral support on her first night of her new job. But the place was so crowded that Piper would most likely be stuck in the kitchen for the entire evening. She was so busy they probably wouldn't even get the chance to wish her good luck.

"Are you telling me nothing odd happened to you today?" Phoebe demanded.

Prue shook her head. "Roger took a project away from me. That was the strangest thing that happened. Actually, it really wasn't so strange when you think about it."

"You didn't freeze time or move anything?" Phoebe pressed on. "Or see the future?"

Prue sipped her coffee. She was getting tired of this conversation. She had just quit her job.

Why should she have to listen to Phoebe's rantings and ravings about witchcraft? "Phoebe, this is ridiculous," Prue said. "We're not witches, okay? And I don't want to talk about it anymore."

Phoebe's drink sat untouched in front of her. "Prue, you've got to listen to me," she pleaded. "We're in terrible danger! Haven't you heard about the killer who's murdering witches?"

"Of course I've heard of him. But since I'm not a witch, I'm not too worried about it. And I should know, shouldn't I? If I'm a witch or not?"

"You *do* know," Phoebe insisted. "You just won't admit it to yourself. We're the Charmed Ones. You, me, and Piper. We're here to fight evil. And we've got to figure out how to summon our powers before a warlock finds us."

"A warlock? Give me a break, Phoebe, will you?" Prue asked. "I think that you've been watching too many horror movies. Besides," Prue added, "if I've got magic powers, why is my life going down the toilet? Wouldn't I use my powers to make things better?"

"You *do* have some kind of power," Phoebe replied. "I'm sure of it. All three of us do."

"All right, Phoebe," Prue said. "If the three of us have powers, then let me see yours."

"I—I can't right now," Phoebe said. "I haven't gotten it yet."

Prue shook her head in disgust. "You're even

flakier than you were before you went to New York. Phoebe, what's up with you?"

Phoebe touched Prue's wrist. "Listen to me," she told her. "I know we're going to get our powers soon. I *know* it."

"*How* do you know it?" Prue asked.

Phoebe hesitated. She glanced behind her to see if anyone was listening, then leaned close to Prue. "Do you remember Grams talking about Melinda Warren?"

Prue nodded. "The first one in the family to come to America. So?"

"I saw her," Phoebe said in a low voice. "In the attic. While I was reading *The Book of Shadows*. I know this is going to sound totally nuts, but she just . . . *appeared* before me."

"As a *ghost?*" Prue asked in disbelief. This was way over the edge—even for Phoebe.

Phoebe nodded. "At first I was frightened. She was all burned and disgusting. Then she told me that we come from a long line of witches, and that I awakened our powers. Mom and Grams were witches, too, but we are the Charmed Ones. The most powerful witches ever!"

Prue stood up and pushed her chair away. She couldn't stand any more of this. "Listen, Phoebe," she snapped. "I really wanted to be here for Piper tonight, but I can't sit here with you another minute."

Phoebe's mouth fell open. "But—"

"No!" Prue held up her hand. "I know you make up these crazy stories just to push my buttons. I'm not going to let you do that to me. Not today."

"Prue, stop," Phoebe whispered. "I'm not making any of this up. I wish I was. Please, please, sit down."

Prue hesitated. Something in Phoebe's voice worried her—a note of desperation.

She's serious, Prue realized. Or upset, or something. Maybe I shouldn't leave her alone here—much as I'd like to.

"Even if you don't want to believe me," Phoebe said, "just once, can't you trust me?"

No, Prue thought as she sat back on her bar stool. Trust was exactly the *last* thing Phoebe deserved, as far as she was concerned.

Prue tried to calm herself down with another sip of coffee. It tasted a little bitter. It needs cream, she decided. She caught sight of a small silver pitcher at the other end of the bar.

"All right, Phoebe," she said. "I'll stay here with you. But let's just get some things straight: I do not have special powers. If I did, you'd be the first to know, okay?" She looked down the bar. "Now pass me the cream."

Prue pointed to the pitcher, and her jaw fell open as she watched the pitcher slowly, deliberately, move along the wooden top of the bar—by itself. It stopped beside her coffee cup.

Prue stared at the pitcher in shock.

Did that just happen? she thought. Or did I imagine it?

She glanced at Phoebe, who was also gaping at the pitcher, stunned. Phoebe saw it move, too, Prue realized. I didn't imagine it.

Heart pounding, Prue eyed the pitcher. The level of milk dropped, as if someone were sucking it up through an invisible straw. At the same time, Prue watched in disbelief as her coffee turned lighter and milkier. The cream swirled around in the cup as if it was stirring itself. Then it bubbled to the top.

Prue shuddered. That had to be a trick, she thought, some kind of brilliant trick. Her stomach gave a nervous lurch.

Phoebe raised her eyebrows in amazement. "You don't have special powers?" she said. "That looked pretty special to me."

CHAPTER 11

Prue stared at the coffee, stunned. Maybe Phoebe was right all along, she thought. Maybe we really do have special powers.

Prue shook her head. No. It had to be a trick. It just had to! "How did you do that, Phoebe?" she demanded.

"Prue, I swear," Phoebe said. "You did that on your own."

Prue dropped her head in her hands. She suddenly felt dizzy. "But how?" she asked. "How did I do it? I didn't feel anything. I wasn't aware of doing anything."

Phoebe shrugged. "I have no idea how it works. It just does."

What does this mean? Prue thought. Images from earlier in the day rushed back to her—

Roger's pen leaking when she was angry with him, and his tie choking him. She remembered pretending to strangle Roger. Then, seconds later he was choking. Some strange power was tightening that tie around his neck, she recalled. Did *I* do that?

Prue's hands began to shake.

"It just . . . I just . . ." Frightened, she grabbed Phoebe by the shoulders. "You mean I can move things with my mind? Telekinesis?"

Phoebe nodded.

"This is so hard to believe," Prue gasped. "We're—we're witches," she whispered.

"I know. It's weird." Phoebe stared off into space. "I wonder which power I'll have. I'd like to be able to freeze time. How cool would that be?"

Prue wished Phoebe had never gone to the attic, had never read that incantation. She shuddered when she remembered how their old spirit board had guided Phoebe up there.

Prue grabbed Phoebe's shot of tequila and drank it down.

"Are you okay?" Phoebe asked.

"No, I'm not okay!" Prue snapped. "You've turned me into a witch!"

"It was probably going to happen sooner or later," Phoebe replied. "You were born a witch. We *all* were. And I think we'd better start learning to deal with that."

Prue's head felt as if it was about to explode.

This was so unreal. She didn't know how to deal with it. She glanced at the front door of the restaurant. She wanted to run right out of this place—away from Phoebe, away from her powers, away from being a witch.

But as she pushed her chair back to leave, she spotted Andy walking into the restaurant. Prue was surprised at how happy she was to see him.

"Hey, Andy," Prue waved him over. "How did you know that I would be here? Are you following me, Inspector?" she asked playfully.

Andy smiled mysteriously. "You know, it's all part of the job. Inspecting and stuff."

You can inspect me any time, Prue thought. The idea gave her a warm flush of pleasure.

"Actually," Andy said, "I'm here to get some take-out."

Phoebe cleared her throat, stood up, and nervously straightened out her clothing.

Why is she acting weird all of a sudden? Prue wondered.

Phoebe took Prue by the hand and guided her off the bar stool. "It was really nice seeing you again," Phoebe said quickly to Andy. She tugged Prue's arm. "I think it's time we left."

"Wait a minute, Phoebe," Prue said. "Again? What's that supposed to mean?"

"We bumped into each other today," Phoebe explained. "I forgot to mention it to you."

She *forgot* to mention it? Prue said to herself. Phoebe bumps into the first boyfriend I've ever had, and she *forgot* to tell me about it? I don't think so, she thought. There's more to it than that.

"Don't go just yet," Andy said. "It's good to see my two favorite Halliwell sisters. Come on, I'll buy you a drink. What do you say?"

Phoebe shook her head no. She pulled some bills from her pocket and threw them onto the bar. "Sorry, Andy, we'll have to take a rain check. We were just leaving."

Then she turned to Prue and whispered in an urgent voice, "I have to talk to you about something important—outside."

A knot slowly churned inside Prue's stomach, and it felt as though her heart had suddenly lodged in her throat. She eyed Phoebe suspiciously. This was exactly how their conversation about Roger had begun. Phoebe had told Prue that she needed to speak with her in private. Then she told Prue that Roger had tricked her into going to his apartment, and that he had tried to seduce her.

Oh, no, Prue thought, glancing at her old boyfriend. Not again.

"Come on, Prue." Phoebe dragged Prue away from Andy. "Let's go."

Prue gave Andy an apologetic look and lifted her hand in a small wave good-bye.

"That's all right," Andy called after them.

"I'll let you go for now, but next time it won't be so easy." He laughed.

Prue reluctantly followed Phoebe out of the restaurant. How many times is she going to do this to me? she wondered.

We finally got away from him, Phoebe thought as she and Prue walked out of the restaurant and onto the sidewalk.

"You were so rude to Andy in there," Prue turned to Phoebe. "Do you want to tell me what's going on between you and him?"

Oh, boy, Phoebe thought as Prue's eyes flashed angrily at her. I know what's on her mind.

"Listen," Phoebe began as they walked toward Prue's car. "It's not what you're thinking. There's nothing going on between me and Andy. I just think it's a little weird that Andy showed up right after you discovered your power."

"What are you talking about? What does Andy have to do with any of this witch stuff?" Prue asked.

"When I was looking in *The Book of Shadows* I saw these wood carvings. They looked like something out of a Bosch painting from the late 1400s," Phoebe explained. "All these terrifying images of three women battling different incarnations of evil."

"Evil fighting evil," Prue replied with a laugh. "That's a twist."

"Not evil fighting evil," Phoebe countered. "*Good* fighting evil. Lots of witches are good, you know."

Prue folded her arms in front of her chest. "What a relief. But what does this have to do with Andy?"

"I'm getting to that," Phoebe told her. They turned the corner into a small parking lot. "But you have to know something. A witch can be good or evil. A good witch follows the Wiccan Rede. 'An it harm none, do what ye will,'" Phoebe recited what she had read. "A bad witch, or a warlock, has two goals: to kill good witches and to steal their powers."

"Okay, wait a minute. What does this have to do with us?" Prue asked Phoebe as they headed toward Prue's red sports car.

"The women in the first wood carving were in slumber, but in the second one they were battling some kind of warlock."

Prue leaned on the door to her car and rolled her eyes. "So?" she replied.

"Melinda Warren told me that once our powers are awakened, warlocks will come after us." Phoebe shook her head. "It's as if they have some kind of radar or something." She placed her hand on Prue's shoulder. "When we were in the dark about our powers we were safe. Not anymore. Warlocks will come after us now, and they look like regular people. They could be anyone, anywhere."

"What does this have to do with Andy?" Prue asked impatiently. "Wait a minute? Are you saying that Andy is a warlock? That's so ridiculous. We've known him most of our lives!"

"But it's possible," Phoebe warned her. "Remember—we just found out yesterday that we're witches, and all of a sudden he pops into our lives again? Besides, he was acting really strangely when I saw him today."

"Where did you see him?" Prue asked.

"At a Wicca store in the Haight. He said he was investigating those witch murders." Phoebe leaned close to Prue and spoke quietly. "But he picked up this ceremonial knife and went into some kind of trance. I freaked out. I thought he was going to kill me right then and there!"

Prue took a few steps away from the car. "But he didn't hurt you, did he?"

"No," Phoebe admitted. "He didn't have time. Someone walked in."

"Look. I'm sure that knife had something to do with the investigation," Prue told her.

Prue doesn't know, Phoebe thought. She wasn't there. She didn't see how freaky Andy had acted.

"Don't you think it's weird that Andy ran into *both* of us on the same day?" Phoebe asked. "After all this time? The day after I awakened our powers?"

Prue frowned. Phoebe watched as this idea seemed to sink in.

"But—" Prue began. "But when I had coffee with him this morning he was fine. We had a great time together. Andy can't be a warlock!"

"Wait a minute," Phoebe said. "*You* saw him this morning. *I* saw him this afternoon. And tonight—" she paused, a terrible thought suddenly hitting her. "And tonight he shows up at the restaurant where Piper works!"

"Phoebe," Prue said. "Piper just got that job today. How could he . . ."

Exactly, Phoebe thought. How *could* he know.

"Piper's in there with Andy now," she said. "We have to go back to Quake. She might be in danger!"

CHAPTER
12

Prue followed Phoebe as they raced back to the restaurant. How could Andy be a warlock? she wondered. Wouldn't I have gotten some sort of clue when we were going out together? Phoebe can't be right. There has to be some kind of logical explanation.

"We can't just burst in there all hysterical," Prue said.

"Okay," Phoebe whispered. "Let's go around to the back. We can probably see Piper through a kitchen window or something."

"Phoebe, I'm sure she's fine," Prue protested, following her sister around back. "Andy wouldn't—"

"Shh!" Phoebe interrupted. "We'll just make sure. If she's fine, then we'll leave."

They snuck up to the window and peered in-side. Prue watched as Piper stood at a steel table, dressed in her chef uniform, talking to a man—Andy!

"He's in there!" Phoebe whispered. "He's talking to her!"

"I can see that, Phoebe," Prue replied, her head beginning to pound.

Prue eyed them carefully. She couldn't catch a glimpse of Andy's face, but Piper was smiling and nodding. Kitchen workers hustled about, chopping vegetables and stirring sauces.

She doesn't look frightened, Prue thought. Actually, she looks pretty calm, considering how busy it is in there. Piper has everything under control.

Prue watched Phoebe stare anxiously through the window. She always gets so carried away, Prue thought.

"I'm sure there's a simple explanation for all this, Phoebe," Prue said. "Maybe Andy comes to Quake all the time. Maybe he's been eating here since *before* Piper got the job. He works hard. He gets hungry. So he's talking to Piper. That doesn't mean he's a warlock."

"But what's he doing in the kitchen?" Phoebe asked. "Customers aren't exactly allowed to get their take-out bags themselves."

"I don't know, Phoebe." Prue's head throbbed with pain. "Maybe Piper saw him and invited him in. Who knows?" She glanced through the window again. Andy breezed out the kitchen's silver double doors with a bag of food. "See?" Prue said. "Piper is fine."

"I guess you're right," Phoebe admitted.

"Can we leave now?" Prue asked. "I want to stop at the pharmacy on the way home. All this witch stuff is giving me a terrible headache."

Prue and Phoebe walked silently back to Prue's car. Andy's not a warlock, Prue told herself. Phoebe may have been right about our powers but she's not right about everything. In fact, she's hardly ever right about anything.

They hopped into Prue's car and drove to the pharmacy. Prue's headache pounded harder with every minute that passed. So I'm a witch, she thought, still bristling at the idea. Fine. I just don't want to think about it anymore. All I care about is making this headache go away.

Inside the pharmacy Prue stalked the aisles, searching for aspirin. Phoebe trotted behind her. It must be in the next aisle, Prue thought, turning a corner.

"Maybe Andy always knew we were witches," Phoebe whispered. "But he had to wait for our powers to be awakened before he could come after us."

Phoebe, shut up, Prue thought irritably. She pressed a finger against her throbbing temple. "I told you. Andy's not a warlock," she whispered back. "He can't be."

"And I told *you* that anybody could be a war-lock—man, woman, child," Phoebe went on. "Anybody, anywhere. Even Andy."

Prue stopped short and whirled around to face her sister. "Thanks for making my headache worse. I need to find the aspirin."

"You know, chamomile tea works great for headaches," Phoebe suggested.

"Not for this one, it won't," Prue shot back. She turned down another aisle, but all she could find was shampoo and hairspray. "Doesn't this pharmacy carry anything besides hair-care products?" she asked.

She stopped at a cash register in the front of the store. "Excuse me. Where do you keep the aspirin?"

The cashier, a teenage boy, didn't even bother to look up from the magazine he was reading. "It's in aisle three," he replied.

Prue marched over to aisle three with Phoebe following close behind.

Prue scanned the rows and rows of cold medicines. Where is the stupid aspirin? she wondered.

"You know, I'm not afraid of our powers," Phoebe continued. "I mean, everyone inherits something from their family. Am I right?"

"Yeah. Money, antiques, maybe a strong disposition," Prue shot back. "That's what *normal* people inherit." She turned back to the shelves. Cough medicine, toothpaste . . . Prue was beginning to feel as though her head would explode.

"Who wants to be normal when we can be special?" Phoebe asked with a smile.

"*I* want to be normal," Prue insisted. "I want my *life* to be normal!" Her head pounded harder—so hard she could almost hear the blood rushing to her brain. She glanced up at the sign at the end of the aisle. "This is aisle three. He said the aspirin was in aisle three, right?"

"But we can't change what's happened," Phoebe replied. "We can't undo our destiny. And we don't really have time to worry about it. We're in danger. We have to learn how to use our powers—fast!"

"Do you see any aspirin?" Prue snapped at her. She wished that Phoebe would just let it rest. Witches, warlocks,—she didn't want to hear any more.

Phoebe peered at a display at the end of the aisle. "I see chamomile tea."

"Look." Prue turned to face her sister. "I just found out that I'm a witch," she said angrily. "And that my sisters are also witches. And that we have powers that will apparently unleash all forms of evil. Evil that is apparently going to come looking for us. So excuse me, Phoebe, but I'm not exactly in a homeopathic mood right now!"

"Then why don't you use your power?"

Phoebe said matter-of-factly. "Move your headache out of your mind."

"Give it up!" Prue shouted—and a bottle of aspirin suddenly flew off the shelf. Prue's hand automatically shot up and and caught it in midair.

Phoebe's eyes widened.

Prue stared at Phoebe for a moment, then gazed at the bottle of aspirin in her hand: extra-strength.

It happened again, she thought, amazed. How? How am I doing this?

"You move things when you're upset," Phoebe said with a smile. "I know it."

"You're crazy," Prue said. "You know, Grams used to joke that she dropped you on your head once when you were a baby. Maybe she wasn't kidding."

"*The Book of Shadows* said our powers would grow," Phoebe added.

"Grow to what?" Prue gripped the bottle of aspirin. She was really upset now.

"Who knows?" Phoebe replied.

Prue stared at her sister. "My powers can't possibly get any stronger. Not if I don't want them to. At least I can control *that*. And I *don't* move things when I'm upset. If anyone can keep emotions in check, I can."

"I'll prove it to you," Phoebe said. "The more upset you get, the stronger your powers are."

This is so childish, Prue thought.

"Ro-ger," Phoebe taunted her with a sing-song voice.

Just the mention of his name caused a familiar anger to grow inside of Prue. She tried to hold it back.

Three more aspirin bottles flew off the shelf and crashed to the floor.

Startled, Prue bent down to scoop them up. That didn't happen because I'm angry with Roger, she told herself. It couldn't have.

"Now let's talk about Dad and see what happens," Phoebe replied.

Dad, Prue thought. Why did Phoebe have to mention him? She struggled to rein in her anger. Prue hated her father more than she hated anything or anyone. "Dad is dead," she said.

"No, he isn't," Phoebe replied. "He moved from New York, but he's very much alive."

"Not to me, he isn't," Prue shot back. "He died the day he left Mom."

"Yeah, right," Phoebe said with a laugh. "He's always been a major button-pusher for you. You're mad that Dad's alive. You're mad I tried to find him, and you're mad that I came back. Dad-Dad-Dad-Dad-Dad-Dad-Dad!"

Prue glared at her sister. She couldn't hold it back any longer. She hated her father, and she hated Phoebe right then for bringing him up!

Anger rushed through her body like a tidal wave.

The entire aisle of medicines, hundreds of

bottles, flew off the pharmacy shelves and crashed to the floor.

"Don't you *dare* talk about Dad to me!" Prue shouted. "You don't remember how you used to cry yourself to sleep after he left. You were too little. I had to sit with you for hours in your bed until you couldn't keep your eyes open! You started thinking that there were monsters everywhere—under your bed, in the basement. So *don't* talk to me about Dad, okay? Because I remember what it was like after he left us. I remember *everything!*"

Prue took a deep breath. Her headache was gone. She felt relaxed, as if she could breathe again for the first time in months. She let out a long exhale.

"Feel better now?" Phoebe asked with a weak smile.

"Lots," Prue replied. She stared at the bottles on the floor. Somehow, this is what I always imagined would happen if I really let my emotions free. But it's okay, she thought, gazing at the mess. It's nothing that can't be cleaned up.

Prue smiled. Her power was already beginning to lose its ability to surprise her—almost as if it was beginning to feel a little . . . normal?

CHAPTER
13

Phoebe sat with Piper at the kitchen table late the next morning. She clutched her cup of coffee and watched the beautiful way the light filtered into the room, casting the kitchen in a warm, sunny glow.

"I'm exhausted," Piper said, rubbing her eyes. She dug her spoon into a bowl of cereal.

"Did you go out with Jeremy after work last night?" Phoebe asked.

Piper shook her head. "No. I was too tired. I didn't get out of Quake until late."

Phoebe wondered if she should tell Piper about Prue and her powers. No, she decided. I'll let Prue tell her.

"Morning, Prue," Piper said sweetly.

Phoebe looked up.

Prue, who was still wearing her pajamas, entered the kitchen. She grabbed a mug and poured herself a cup of coffee.

"You're up later than usual," Phoebe said to Prue as she strolled into the kitchen.

"No need to wake up early," Prue replied dragging her feet to the table. "No job, remember?"

Piper's mouth fell open. "When did *this* happen?" she asked.

"Yesterday," Prue replied. "Roger stole the credit for a project I was working on, so I quit."

"I guess I'll be supporting the three of us from now on, huh?" Piper said with a laugh. "But really, I'm glad that you stood up for your principles. You'll find something else before you know it. When one door closes, another one opens right up."

"That theory doesn't exactly work for me," Phoebe complained. "Doors have been slamming in my face everywhere I go. I can never keep a job."

"You'll find a good job once you figure out what it is that you really want to do," Prue said. "You just have to be patient, Phebes. Give it time."

Wow. Prue called me Phebes, Phoebe thought. It's been a long time since she called me that. She seems so calm this morning. Maybe Prue's powers have changed her for the better, she decided. I wonder when she's going to tell Piper about it.

Piper cleared her throat. "Now that you're both here, I have something to tell you guys."

"What is it?" Phoebe asked. Piper sounded serious.

Piper glanced from Phoebe to Prue. "Well, . . ." she said slowly. "Something weird happened to me yesterday. I was cooking my audition meal when Chef Moore burst into the kitchen," Piper explained. "He said my time was up, but my port sauce wasn't ready. I didn't know what to do. I needed more time. I knew if he tasted that pasta sauce before I put the port in, I'd never get the job."

"Couldn't you tell him you needed another minute?" Prue asked.

"It was too late," Piper said. "He'd already taken some pasta and was about to put it in his mouth. Then I told him to stop." Piper paused. "And he did."

"That's great," Phoebe said. "I hear that those French chefs can be kind of temperamental."

"No, that's not it." Piper waved her hands and then stopped. She placed them under the table. "You don't get it. He just *stopped*. And so did everything else in the room. Even the water stopped boiling. It sat in the pot with these—these weird, frozen bubbles, perfectly still." She glanced at Phoebe. "Do you think . . . do you think *I* did it? Is this what you were talking about, Phoebe? Do I have the power to stop time?" She dropped her head in her hands. "Am I really a witch?"

"Don't worry, Piper," Prue said, rubbing Piper's back for comfort. "You're not alone. I can move things with my mind. Phoebe was with me when it happened."

Piper shook her head. "You're kidding, right?"

"No. It's true," Phoebe admitted. "She trashed aisle three of the pharmacy. Bottles were flying off the shelves—all by themselves."

"You were right all along, Phebes," Piper breathed. "But it's so hard to believe!"

"Melinda said the third power will be to see the future," Phoebe said. "That will be my power, I guess. Wow." Pretty ironic, she thought, since Prue was always saying how I have no sense of the future, no vision. But when am I going to get my power? she thought, worried.

"I've got to get my power before a warlock attacks," she said out loud. "We don't know who the warlock will be, or how to fight him. If I could see the future, maybe it would give us a clue."

Piper stared at her. "Warlocks? Attack? What are you talking about?"

"Didn't you hear anything I said to you yesterday morning?" Phoebe asked. "We're in danger! Warlocks want to steal our powers—

by killing us! Those women who were killed, were killed by a warlock. The women were witches! And every time the killer murders one he gets stronger, because he takes that witch's power."

Piper gripped her coffee cup until her knuckles turned white. "How do we recognize a warlock?" she asked.

"We can't," Prue explained. "Phoebe says anyone could be a warlock." She glanced at Phoebe, who slunk down in her seat, knowing what was coming next. "That's why we had to leave Quake early last night," Prue continued. "Phoebe got a little paranoid. She thought Andy was a warlock."

Piper laughed. "Andy? Give me a break. He's a detective."

"I have a lot of good reasons to suspect him," Phoebe insisted. "You guys don't seem to get it. From now on, we can't trust anyone but one another."

"What about Jeremy?" Prue said. "Could he be a warlock?"

"Jeremy?" Piper scoffed. "No way. He's the nicest guy I've ever met."

"Piper, you never know," Phoebe warned.

"So anybody in the world could be out to get us?" Piper asked. "I can't handle that. What about the paperboy? Could it be him? Or the deli guy?"

Phoebe nodded.

"Or, let's say, Roger?" Piper said, looking at Prue.

"I wouldn't put anything past Roger," Prue said. "But I doubt he's a warlock. He's evil but not that evil."

"Look, the point is, we don't know where the evil is going to come from," Phoebe said. "So we all have to be very careful, okay?"

Piper and Prue exchanged glances. They weren't used to taking orders from their baby sister. But they nodded, and Piper said, "Okay."

"What was Andy saying to you last night, anyway?" Phoebe asked.

Piper raised an eyebrow. "How do you know he was talking to me last night? I was in the kitchen the whole time."

Oops. "We sort of spied on you," Phoebe admitted. "Through the kitchen window."

"Are you guys nuts?" Piper shook her head in disbelief.

"We had to do it," Phoebe explained. "We thought you were in danger. We thought Andy might try to hurt you!"

"But when we saw that everything was all right, we left," Prue added.

"So, what *was* Andy saying to you, anyway?" Phoebe repeated.

"He just wanted Prue's number," Piper replied. "He lost it. I told him we were all living at Grams' house again."

"You told him where we live?" Phoebe cried.

"Phoebe, it doesn't matter," Prue cut in. "I told him myself when I first ran into him. Of course, at the time I had no idea he could be a warlock. I didn't even know such a thing existed." She scanned the kitchen. "Hey, did anyone bring in the paper?"

"Not yet," Phoebe replied.

"I'll get it," Prue pushed her chair away from the table and left the kitchen, taking her coffee with her. "Got to start looking for a new job!" she called from the hallway.

"Why don't you get a job with a moving company," Piper called out. "You could move whole houses full of furniture without lifting a finger!"

Prue popped her head back in the kitchen. "Ha ha," she said, and disappeared out the door again.

Phoebe sighed, suddenly feeling restless. "I've got to get out of here for a little while," she said, standing. "I can't stop thinking about warlocks. It's starting to drive me crazy. I need to clear my head."

"All right, but I'll probably be gone when you get back," Piper said. "I have to get to the restaurant a little early to talk about the specials. And don't freak out if I don't come home tonight. I'm seeing Jeremy later. Okay?"

Phoebe stopped in her tracks and turned to

face Piper. "Tell me again. How long have you known this guy?"

"Phoebe . . ."

"Okay, okay." She pointed her finger at her sister. "But be careful."

"Yes, Mom," Piper said with a smile.

"Good luck," Phoebe said, and hurried out of the kitchen. She picked up her backpack near the front door and left the house.

Prue and Piper aren't taking this warlock business seriously, she thought. And they're making me feel a little paranoid. But I've been right about everything, so far.

Prue has a power and so does Piper. And soon the evil will come, she thought, unlocking her bike from the porch. She carried her bike down the steps that led to the street and hopped on.

An image of Andy filtered into her mind. It's not as if I *want* him to be a warlock, she told herself. But I just can't stop thinking about the way he held that jeweled knife.

CHAPTER 14

Prue gazed at herself in the mirror as she clipped on an earring. I don't look any different, she thought. And I don't feel any different. Not really.

But I am different.

She studied her reflection. She was wearing a dark blue wrap dress, elegant but not too dressy, and strappy blue sandals. She was getting ready to meet Andy for lunch.

He'd called right after Piper had left for work. Phoebe was still on her bike ride.

Good, Prue thought. Phoebe won't be around to talk me out of seeing Andy.

After all of Phoebe's warnings about warlocks, Prue was a little hesitant about meeting Andy this afternoon. But she decided that she had to go. She couldn't lock herself away now that she knew she was a witch, right? Besides, she knew Andy intimately. He couldn't hide a secret that big from her, could he?

Prue hurried downstairs. She checked herself once more in the mirror by the door. Then she locked the house, got into her car, and drove downtown to meet Andy.

She felt as if butterflies were dancing around in her stomach when she entered the small bistro.

Stop being so nervous, she told herself. Phoebe's wrong about Andy. There's no way he's a warlock. But why did Phoebe have to put that stupid idea into my head?

Her doubts melted away as soon as she saw him waiting for her.

Andy rose when Prue approached the booth.

He's got such an honest face, she thought as she sat beside him. I've always liked that about him.

"Hey," he said, pecking her on the cheek. "What'll you have?" he asked when the waiter appeared.

"A glass of white wine," Prue told the waiter.

"So, anything new since I last saw you?" he asked. "Let's see, the last time I saw you would be, yesterday?"

Prue grinned to cover her thoughts. Actually, a lot was new since yesterday. A whole lot. But what can I say? I'm a witch now? I don't think so.

Then she remembered something she could tell him. "Well, one thing that's new is I'm out of a job," she said. "I quit yesterday."

Andy's eyebrows shot up in surprise. "Why?"

"Roger was my boss," Prue explained. "Ever since I broke off the engagement he's been giving me a hard time. Yesterday was just the last straw."

"It's probably for the best. It's not easy to work with someone you've been involved with."

"Tell me about it," Prue said. "But it was such a great job. I really loved it."

Andy put an arm around her. "Don't worry," he said softly. "You'll get another job—easy. A better one, too. I know you, Prue. And I know nothing can stop you from rising to the top. That's where you belong."

She sank into Andy's shoulder, taking in the comfort he offered her. It felt so good to lean on someone. For once she didn't have to be the strong one.

When Prue's drink arrived, she sat up to take a sip. "How is the murder investigation going?" she asked. "Are you any closer to finding the person who's killing all those women?"

Andy shook his head. "The guy is really good. We're stumped. We're trying to figure out how to guess who the next victim will be. But aside from combing the tattoo parlors, we have no way of knowing."

Prue shifted uncomfortably on her seat, thinking of Phoebe. Their powers had been awakened, and warlocks were going to come after them. We could be the next victims, Prue thought.

She shuddered and cast a glance at Andy.

"Prue, are you all right?" Andy asked.

"Sure," she said, smiling weakly. Maybe I should tell him, she thought. I should tell him I'm a witch. It could help the investigation.

"It's just that these Wiccan rituals are so strange," Andy said. "I don't quite understand what they're supposed to accomplish. It's all so weird. It's hard to believe that there are so many people who get off on this stuff."

Prue pulled away a little. He'd never understand if I told him, she realized. No. I can't tell him. Not yet, anyway.

What would he think of me if he knew I was a witch? she wondered. Would he think I was crazy? Would he be afraid of me? He'd probably run screaming in the opposite direction, Prue thought.

"Prue? Are you sure you're okay? You look as if your mind is somewhere else."

"I'm okay, Andy," she assured him. "Everything's fine and perfectly normal. I promise."

"No," Andy replied. "It's not. Something's going on."

Prue remained silent.

"Something must have happened to you yesterday," Andy went on. "You're not the same."

Prue tried to think of some clever way to reply, but she couldn't. "Um, what makes you say that, Andy?"

"You're different. It's as if you don't trust me. You used to tell me everything. So tell me now. What's happened to you?"

He tried to put his arm around Prue's shoulders, but Prue snaked away. She was suddenly uncomfortable sitting next to him. *Very* uncomfortable.

Prue glanced around the restaurant, looking for other customers. Weird. It was lunchtime, and the place was practically empty.

"What's going on with you?" Andy pressed on.

"You know what, Andy? I've got to go," Prue stood up. "I just remembered something. Could you let me out of the booth?"

"But we haven't even ordered yet." Andy stood up and stepped out of the way.

Prue slid out of the booth. "I'm sorry, Andy. I'll talk to you later."

"Prue—wait. . . ."

Prue felt Andy's eyes on her as she quickly left the restaurant. As she rushed down the sidewalk, she glanced back to see if he was following her.

Andy stood at the door to the restaurant staring at her.

They locked eyes for a moment. Then Prue turned the corner and raced to her car.

The message light on the answering machine was blinking when Prue got home. She tossed her car keys on the hall table and pressed the button.

"Prue, it's Roger." Prue rolled her eyes at the smarmy sound of his voice. Now what? she wondered.

"I've been looking for you," he said. "And I'll find you. You can't get away from me that easily."

Prue felt a chill as she listened to the message. What did Roger mean? Was he threatening her?

"I need you," Roger continued. "I need your—"

Click. Roger hung up. Prue stood in the hallway, staring at the answering machine, shaking. What was Roger going to say? Why did he hang up?

Phoebe's voice ran through her mind: Warlocks are coming to kill us. And they could be anyone.

Anyone, Prue thought. Like Andy. Or like Roger?

Phoebe pumped her legs as she struggled to ride up a steep San Francisco hill. She loved riding her bicycle. The physical exercise relaxed her, and it could make her forget almost anything.

She huffed as she neared the top of the hill. The fun part is just ahead, Phoebe thought.

Then she felt a sudden dizziness that almost knocked her off her bike. I'm probably just working my body too hard, Phoebe told herself. I should slow down a little. I'm not used to the hills anymore.

A bright light flashed into Phoebe's eyes. She felt a jolt of electricity run through her body, and she gasped, overcome with fear. What is it? she wondered. She closed her eyes, and a scene unfolded in her mind:

Two teenage boys on in-line skates. No helmets.

Going fast. Very fast.

Jumping over curbs, weaving in and out.

A car rounds a corner. A black car.

A horn honks. Tires screech. The car swerves.

Too late. Too late.

The car hits the boys.

Blood in the street.

Dripping from their cracked heads . . .

The images disappeared. Phoebe blinked and shook her head to clear it. She stood in the street, half-balanced on her bike, a little shaken.

What was that? she wondered. What just happened?

She stared at the landscape, the houses around her. It was different from what she had seen in her mind. She didn't see any teenage boys or a black car.

But the scene felt so real, she thought. I saw those two boys get hurt!

Was that a vision? she wondered, catching her breath. If it was, she thought, I've got to do something. I've got to save those boys!

She glanced around, searching for signs of the skaters or the black car. Then she jumped on her bike and pedaled furiously, frantically searching.

No black car. No boys.

She crouched as her bike flew down a hill. The wind rushed at her face. Her hair whipped behind her. I've got to find them, she thought, scanning the street ahead of her. Then she saw it—a black car in the distance, heading toward her, speeding. Phoebe's heart started to pound.

Is that it? she wondered. Is that the car?

As she neared a bend in the road, she spotted two skaters, zipping up and down curbs. She gasped.

Her eyes darted from the car to the boys and back again.

They don't see the car. It's going to hit them! Phoebe pedaled as hard as she could.

"No, wait!" she screamed at the boys. She raced ahead to try to cut the boys off—to try to keep them from skating in front of that car.

She swerved in front of them.

The two boys turned to avoid her.

Phoebe swerved again, lost control of her bike, and fell to the ground. She winced as a searing pain shot through her left shoulder.

Tires screeched.

Phoebe looked up just in time to see the grille of the black car heading straight toward her—too fast to stop.

"Nooooooooo!"

CHAPTER
15

Prue hurried into the hospital emergency room. Please, please, please, she thought as she pushed her way through the lines of waiting people to the front desk. Please let Phoebe be okay.

A man stood at the nurse's desk, his back to her. She didn't wait for him to finish his conversation with the nurse. She planted herself beside him and interrupted.

"I'm looking for my sister Phoebe Halliwell," she said to the admitting nurse.

"Just one second, please," the nurse said, annoyed.

The man at the desk turned to look at Prue.

Prue gasped. It was Andy.

Again, Prue thought. Her shoulder muscles tensed.

"Prue! What's the matter? Is Phoebe all right?"

"I don't know," Prue said. "She had some kind of accident." She paused and glanced at him nervously. "What are you doing here?"

"Murder investigation," Andy replied. "The Wicca killer. I'm here to check out the body of victim number seven."

There was an awkward silence. Andy turned back to the nurse. "Do you know when Dr. Gordon will be available?" he asked her.

"About twenty minutes," the nurse replied. "You can wait outside his office if you'd like."

"Thanks," Andy said. He turned to face Prue. "What happened this afternoon?" he asked. "Why did you get so freaked out?"

Prue bristled at the edge of anger in his voice. That's not the Andy I remember, she thought. He never used to speak angrily to me. She didn't know what to say.

"Prue, talk to me," Andy pleaded. He softened his voice this time, gazing at her with his warm hazel eyes.

Maybe I'm overreacting, she thought as the warmth in his eyes melted her. Maybe all this witch stuff is confusing me. She desperately wanted to tell Andy her secret. Maybe Andy could help her somehow. She wanted to trust someone—to trust him.

No, she told herself. Phoebe's probably right. I can't trust anyone.

She caught Andy staring at her, trying to figure out what she was thinking. She looked away.

"I just hope my sister's okay," she finally said.

"Prue." Piper walked down the hallway with Jeremy.

"What's going on?" Prue ran over to them. "Have you seen Phoebe? Is she all right?"

"She's fine," Piper assured her. "She fell off her bike. A car nearly hit her, but it swerved away just in time. The doctor said she was very lucky. No broken bones. Just a few scrapes and bruises. She'll be out of X-ray in a minute."

"Oh, good," Prue said, relieved.

Andy appeared behind her. "Hi, Piper."

"Hi, Andy." Piper shot a glance at Prue, and Prue understood what it meant: What's he doing here? Piper smiled stiffly at Andy and added, "Nice to see you again. This is my boyfriend, Jeremy." She turned to Jeremy and added, "Jeremy, this is an old friend of Prue's—Andy Trudeau."

Andy shook Jeremy's hand. "Good to meet you."

"Same here," Jeremy said.

"Well, I've got to get back to the restaurant," Piper said. "Are you going to be all right, Prue?" Piper glanced nervously at Andy.

She nodded reassuringly at her sister and said, "I'll be fine. I'll drive Phoebe home."

"Good," Piper replied. "Jeremy's taking me out for dinner later—so don't wait up tonight." Piper waved as she walked out of the emergency room. Prue felt a tiny pang in her heart as she watched Jeremy take Piper's hand.

I wish I had someone like Jeremy, she thought. Someone who'd be there for me. Someone I can trust.

She glanced at Andy. She liked him so much, but could she trust him? She felt a little dizzy thinking about it. Two days ago she would have trusted him without a second's hesitation. But now her life had turned upside down in a single day.

"So," Andy said. "I'm glad to hear Phoebe's okay. The doctor I'm waiting to see won't be free for a little while. What do you say I buy you a cup of coffee?"

Prue hesitated. She looked at Andy's handsome face and remembered how crazy she used to be about him. She could imagine being crazy about him again.

But at the same time, she was still afraid. With all these murders going on, and so many unanswered questions . . . And she hadn't seen Andy in years, until recently. Who was he, anyway? She realized she didn't really know him anymore.

"Thanks again for dinner," Piper said, leaning close to Jeremy. She held onto a small box of fortune cookies as they sat in his parked car.

"You're welcome," Jeremy replied, putting his arm around her. "Of course, the food doesn't compare with anything you make."

Piper smiled, then kissed him. *I've never known any guy who tried so hard to please me,* she thought. *It's almost scary. Why me? Why does he love* me *so much?*

He kissed her again, and she felt as if she'd melt right into the seat of the car.

On the other hand, she thought when she came up for air, *who cares why he loves me? I just should bask in all this attention and be grateful.*

"Piper," Jeremy murmured, gazing into her eyes. "What was going on with Phoebe yesterday?"

"Phoebe?" Piper pulled away slightly. "What do you mean?"

"Well, I couldn't stop thinking about it. She said something to you about having special powers. What was she talking about?"

Piper's insides froze up a little. She wasn't sure she should talk about her powers to anyone, not even Jeremy. "Oh, that," she replied. "That was nothing."

Jeremy kissed her forehead and brushed away her bangs. "But Phoebe seemed really serious."

What's with him? Piper wondered, sitting up a little straighter in the car seat. *Why won't he let this go?*

"Even if I could tell you, you would never believe me," she said, trying to keep the worry from her voice.

"Of course I'd believe you. I'd believe anything you told me." He gently stroked her cheek. "Come on."

Piper felt a little uncomfortable. She wanted to tell Jeremy everything. But what if she told him she was a witch—what would he do? He'd probably run for his life, she thought. She popped open the box of fortune cookies. "Here, let's see what your fortune is."

"Okay." Jeremy took a cookie and snapped it open. He pulled out a small piece of paper. " 'Soon you will be on top,' " he read aloud.

Piper smiled. "It doesn't say that."

"Yes it does." Jeremy laughed.

"Let me see," Piper said snatching the fortune from his hand and read it. " 'Of the world. Soon you will be on top of the world.' " She playfully tossed the paper at her boyfriend.

Jeremy pulled her into an embrace, and they kissed once again. Piper never wanted to leave his arms. He was so sensitive—he knew just how to touch her.

"I want to know everything about you, Piper," Jeremy whispered into her ear. "I've never met anyone as incredible as you."

Piper smiled. "I've never met anyone as incredible as you either," she said. Maybe I should tell him, she thought. After all, if we're ever going to be close—really close—he'd have to find out eventually.

She took a deep breath and started slowly. "Jeremy, has anything strange or unexplainable ever happened to you?"

"Sure," he said. "It's called luck. Or fate. Some call it miracles. Why?"

"Well, Phoebe thinks we have special powers," Piper admitted. "The three of us—Phoebe, Prue, and I."

She studied Jeremy's face. How was he taking this so far? At that moment she thought he just looked curious.

"What kind of special powers?" he asked. "You mean, like your fabulous cooking?" He nuzzled her and added, "Your wonderful kissing?"

Piper shook her head. "No. I mean *really* special." She paused. The next part was hard to say.

"I didn't believe Phoebe," Piper continued. "But then something weird happened at Quake—at my audition."

She glanced at him. He nodded, paying close attention.

"It—it was as if I stopped time," she told him. She explained everything—how she didn't have time to finish preparing her meal, and how she froze Chef Moore before he could taste it. "I know it's hard to believe. But it really happened!"

Jeremy raised his eyebrows and pulled away.

Piper hugged herself as if she felt cold. Talking about her power made her nervous. She still wasn't sure how it worked, or what it meant for her future. She stole a glance at Jeremy. How was he taking this news? Was he freaking out?

Piper was shaking now. She'd been so busy at work, she hadn't had time to let all this sink in. Now that she thought about it, it was starting to scare her.

I'm so glad I have Jeremy, she thought as he stroked her hair, trying to soothe her. He's taking this well—so far, anyway. He looked perfectly calm. "Do you think I'm crazy?" she asked.

"No," he whispered. "Everything's going to be okay. And I want you to know, nothing you can tell me will scare me away. I'll love you no matter what. But you know, you've been working really hard lately. You've been under a lot of stress."

He doesn't believe me, she thought. "You're right. It was just temporary insanity." She forced a laugh.

"You're shaking." Jeremy took her hand. "Listen, I think I know something that will calm you down."

He started the car and pulled away.

"Where are we going?" Piper asked.

"You'll see. I'm taking you to an awesome spot. The view there is gorgeous. It will make you feel much better."

Piper relaxed into her seat. What would I do without him? she wondered.

They sat quietly as Jeremy drove across town. He pulled onto a small, dark road. Piper sat up, trying to see where they were headed.

The road passed through a deserted industrial area.

"Where are we going?" she asked.

"I want to show you the old Bowing Building," Jeremy answered. "It's got an amazing view of the Bay Bridge."

"Oh." She didn't like the looks of this part of town. So dark. Nobody around anywhere. Why is he taking me here? she wondered, her heart starting to race slightly. It seems a little strange.

Jeremy stopped the car in front of a huge, deserted warehouse. "This is it," he said, getting out of the car.

"This is it?" Piper echoed. She gazed up at the dark, hulking building. It looked as if it might crumble to the ground any second.

Jeremy got out of the car and started for the door. "Come on, Piper," he urged. "There's nothing to be afraid of."

Piper reluctantly climbed out of the car and followed him. She jumped back as Jeremy kicked the warehouse door open. The rusty hinges creaked.

Piper peered inside. The building was dark, lit only by the streetlight outside, and it smelled damp and musty. This is not very romantic, she thought.

"I'm sorry," she told him. "I don't care how amazing the view is. I'm not going in there."

Jeremy grinned mischievously.

"I mean it," she insisted.

He took her arm. "You have to come inside. I've got a surprise for you."

He led her into the building, stopping in front of a wire gate leading to an elevator. He wrenched open the gate. "After you," he said, motioning inside.

Piper hesitated.

"Go on," Jeremy said. "It's perfectly safe. I promise."

Piper stepped inside the elevator. Jeremy followed and closed the gate. Then he pressed a button and a light flickered on. The elevator roared to life. With lots of clanging and banging, it began to rise.

"You are going to love this," Jeremy said. "You'll tell Phoebe and Prue about it the moment you see them. And Prue's friend Andy. He's a detective, right?"

Piper froze. "I never mentioned that," she said. "I never told you Andy was a detective." She took a step away from Jeremy, glancing at him nervously. "How did you know that?"

"Oops," Jeremy said.

The elevator light flickered, then went out.

Piper heard the sound of metal scraping

metal. The elevator jarred to a stop. Her heart was beating fast now. "What's happening?" she cried.

No reply.

"Jeremy?" Piper asked.

The light flickered back on again. Jeremy stood in front of her, a wide grin plastered on his face. In his hand he held a jeweled, double-sided gold knife.

Piper's heart pounded. This has to be a joke, she told herself. "What is that?"

Jeremy grinned even wider. "This is your surprise."

CHAPTER
16

Piper shrank back as Jeremy took a step toward her. "Jeremy," she said firmly. "Stop it. You're scaring me."

Clutching the knife, he took another step toward her. "Good," he replied. "You're supposed to be scared."

Piper's back pressed against the elevator wall. No, she thought. This can't be happening! "Cut it out, Jeremy," she demanded. "I'm serious."

"So am I," Jeremy said. His voice suddenly sounded different. Harder. Crueler.

Piper cowered as Jeremy came closer.

"I've waited six months for this moment," Jeremy told her. Now his voice changed completely. It grew deeper—almost metallic-sounding. It echoed with evil.

Piper cringed as he caressed her cheek with his hand.

"Six months," he repeated. "Ever since your grandmother went into the hospital."

Piper was confused. She'd met Jeremy when Grams was in the hospital, but what did that have to do with anything?

"I've known for quite some time now that the moment the old witch croaked, all your powers would be released," Jeremy continued. "Now the time is here."

Piper struggled to take in what Jeremy was saying. So, he knew, she realized. He knew all along about our powers—even before *we* did. And he pretended to be my boyfriend so he could stay close to me and my sisters.

The terror grew inside her as she realized that Phoebe was right.

Piper flattened her body against the elevator wall. A way to get out, she thought. I have to find a way out of here!

"I knew your powers would reveal themselves the moment the three of you were together again," Jeremy growled. "All I had to do was wait for Phoebe to return. Now the rest is easy."

The knife blade glinted in the fluorescent light. Piper's head swooned as it all sank in. He's going to kill me! she thought, panicking. "You killed all those women!" she cried.

"Not women," Jeremy sneered. "Witches."

"Why?" Piper demanded. Keep him talking, she thought as her heart thudded in her chest.

"I'll show you why," Jeremy said. He raised his free hand. Flames sparked from his fingertips.

Piper screamed. He had the power to light a fire at the touch of his finger!

"It was the only way to get their powers," he explained. "I stole the power of fire from one of the witches I killed. She didn't even put up a fight." Jeremy gave a deep, hollow laugh. "Now I'm more powerful than I've ever been before."

"You're—you're a warlock," Piper murmured.

"Now you're catching on." Jeremy grinned. "And once I get the powers of the Charmed Ones, no one will be able to stop me! Don't you wish you knew how to handle your power right about now?"

Come on, she coaxed herself. You can do it. Freeze time. Do it! Do it!

Piper concentrated as hard as she could, but nothing happened.

Jeremy was right, she realized. I don't really understand how my power works yet. She glanced around the elevator, searching for a way out. Please, she thought. A trapdoor—anything!

"Hmm," Jeremy said. "Where should I kill you? Here or on the roof, with the beautiful vision of the Bay Bridge in front of us?" He pressed a button, and the elevator slowly rattled toward the top of the building.

Piper breathed with relief. Maybe once they were on the roof she would have a chance to escape.

Jeremy smiled at Piper. "I think—*here*," he said and stopped the elevator between floors.

Piper gaped at him in terror. She screamed as his blue eyes changed to bloodred.

She threw herself against the elevator door, trying to escape. "Let me out!" she screamed. "Somebody, help!"

Jeremy grabbed her roughly by the shirt and spun her around.

His mouth split into the most evil grin Piper had ever seen.

He raised the golden knife high over his head.

Piper screamed as Jeremy plunged the knife toward her chest.

CHAPTER
17

Noooo!" Piper wailed. "Jeremy, stop!" She squeezed her eyes shut. She waited for the knife to rip through her skin and tear into her heart. But it didn't.

She opened her eyes to see the knife frozen right under her chin.

Jeremy stood stiffly over her, holding the knife, completely still. His face was contorted into an evil grimace.

Piper gasped for breath. I did it, she thought. She didn't know how, but she had frozen Jeremy just in time to save her life.

I've got to get out of here, she thought frantically. I don't know how long this will last.

She tried to pull away from Jeremy, but his

157

grip on her shirt was frozen, too. She couldn't get away!

In a panic, she yanked at the front of her shirt. Then she grabbed his hand. Shaking, she peeled his fingers off the shirt, one at a time.

She was free.

She glanced around the elevator, searching for a way to escape. "Stay calm," she told herself. "Think. Think!"

Piper wrenched open the cage-like metal door. The elevator was stuck between two floors. Below her, all she saw was darkness. She could try to jump down there, but she didn't know how far it was or what she would land on. Over her head, just in reach, was the next floor up. I've got to climb up, she decided quickly. She grabbed the floor above and hoisted herself up. Almost there, she thought as she wriggled her body onto the rough cement. Almost . . .

Piper gasped when she heard the elevator roar to life. No, she thought. Not yet! She glanced back and caught a glimpse of Jeremy's bloodred eyes.

He clasped a hand onto her ankle.

"Noooo!" Piper yelled, kicking him.

Jeremy roared in anger. He grabbed her leg and pulled hard.

Piper felt herself sliding back into the elevator car. Her fingernails scratched at the cement floor. Jeremy's hands tugged on her, moving up her legs, pulling her closer.

She felt along the floor for something, anything, to hold onto. Her fingers touched something. A piece of wood. She wrapped her hands around it.

With a final tug, Jeremy yanked her down. She tumbled back into the elevator, landing hard on the floor.

"No!" she screamed.

Jeremy raised the knife again.

Piper leaped to her feet. She lifted the wooden two-by-four over her head and slammed it down on his head as hard as she could.

Jeremy dropped the knife. His eyes rolled back into his head.

He slumped to the floor, unconscious.

Piper climbed back up and hurled herself out of the elevator. She glanced back at Jeremy and shuddered.

He's unconscious, she thought, gasping for breath. But how long will he be out? How long until he comes after me?

She bolted out of the warehouse, running for her life.

CHAPTER
18

Phoebe woke to her dark bedroom. Prue had driven her home from the hospital after the accident. Phoebe wasn't badly hurt, but she was pretty shaken. She'd gone straight to bed and slept for what seemed like hours.

"The boys," she whispered to herself, remembering why she had gotten into that accident. "They're safe." And it was all because of my power to see the future, she thought. I saved their lives!

Phoebe glanced at the clock on her night table. It was almost midnight. Feeling a little hungry, she decided to fix herself a snack.

She flicked on the hall lights, then the stair lights, then the foyer lights. I wonder where everybody is?

Then Phoebe remembered that Piper had a date with Jeremy. Piper had said that she might not come home that night. But Prue? Where was she? Phoebe hoped she wasn't out with Andy.

Phoebe jumped when the front door slammed open. "Prue! Phoebe!" she heard Piper cry.

"Piper! What's wrong?" Prue asked, emerging from the dark living room. Piper had rushed into the house, breathless. Her clothes were dirty and shredded. Phoebe noticed a bruise on her arm.

"Quick! Lock the doors!" Piper cried. "Check the windows! We don't have much time!"

Phoebe hurried to the front door and locked it. "What happened? What's wrong?" The panic rose in her voice.

Piper grabbed her by the shoulders. "Phoebe—in *The Book of Shadows*, did it say how to get rid of a warlock?"

"Who is it?" Prue's voice shook. "Is it Andy?"

"No. It's Jeremy. He tried to kill me! With one of those knives you were talking about. Double-sided, the jeweled handle—the same knife the other women were killed with. He's the killer! He's a warlock!"

Phoebe shut the living room windows and locked them.

Prue raced to the phone in the parlor. "I'm calling the police," she said, picking up the receiver.

"And tell them what?" Piper asked. "That we're witches? That some freak with powers beyond comprehension is trying to kill us? Even if the cops did come, they'd be no match for Jeremy, and we'd be next."

Phoebe stood by the front door, trembling. This is it, she thought. The first warlock is here. But even if we defeat Jeremy, he won't be the last.

Prue placed the receiver back in its cradle. "Phoebe, go get *The Book of Shadows*."

Phoebe raced upstairs and ran straight to the table where the magical book lay. She frantically flipped through its pages.

There's got to be something in here that will help us, she thought desperately. Why didn't Melinda Warren at least give me a clue?

She stopped at a page in the middle of the book. Written in elaborate scroll, the words seemed to be a recipe, yet the ingredients were kind of odd.

It's some kind of spell, Phoebe realized. And it looks like—maybe—it could kill a warlock.

She hurried downstairs.

"I think I found the answer," she called to her sisters. "Come up to the attic—quick! It's our only hope!"

I can't believe I'm doing this, Prue thought as she sat at a low, round table in the attic. Phoebe and Piper were with her, preparing a spell that Phoebe had found in *The Book of Shadows*.

Prue read through the recipe and shook her head. They were about to cast their first spell, and they had to hurry.

Prue lay the book open on the wooden floor. Then she rose to help Phoebe and Piper light the circle of white candles they had placed around the table.

When they finished, Phoebe crossed the room to the light switch. "Ready?" she asked.

Here we go, Prue thought, taking a deep breath. She nodded, and Phoebe flicked off the lights.

The three sisters took their places around the table.

Prue watched as the flames cast eerie shadows on the walls behind her sisters.

In the middle of the table stood a flat copper bowl with candles of all shapes and sizes mixed with oil and spices. Phoebe had rummaged frantically through the house until she found nine candles to put in the pot.

Prue checked the spell in *The Book of Shadows* once again. "Okay," she said. "We've anointed the nine candles with the oils and spices. And we've placed them in the pot to burn. Right?"

"Wait!" Piper cried. "I only counted eight!"

Phoebe held up a tiny, striped candle. "You forgot this one."

"A birthday candle?" Piper asked.

"Grams was low on witch supplies," Phoebe replied.

Prue rolled her eyes. This is just great, she thought. If we have to do all this witch stuff, at least we should do it right.

Phoebe lit the birthday candle and used it to light the other eight candles in the pot. Soon the pot glowed with the light of nine burning candles. "What's next?" she asked.

Prue glanced at the book. "Next we'll need the poppet."

"Got it," said Piper. She held up a small doll she'd quickly carved out of soap.

"Okay, we're set," Prue said. "We can cast the spell."

"Wait a minute. The book says I have to separate Jeremy from my soul first," Piper said. She grabbed some of the roses Jeremy had given her and placed them on top of the doll. "Your love will wither and depart," she chanted. "From my life and from my heart."

Prue watched as Piper pressed the rose thorns deep into the doll's stomach. She struggled with her common sense. A voice in her head kept saying that this couldn't possibly work.

But Prue knew she'd have to learn to let another voice inside her speak, too. The voice that told her there were powers at work in the world far beyond logic and sense—powers that were beyond comprehension.

Piper held the poppet over the pot. "Let me be, Jeremy," she chanted. "And go away forever."

Piper dropped the poppet and roses into the fiery pot. The smoky flames licked at the soap and flowers.

Prue watched the poppet burn. "Let's hope this works," she said.

Jeremy woke up to find himself on the elevator floor, his head throbbing. What happened? he wondered. Then he remembered. Piper had knocked him out with a two-by-four.

He leaped to his feet, roaring with fury. "That *witch!*" he cried, springing out of the elevator.

He ran out of the warehouse and sprinted down the empty street in a rage. Suddenly, an excruciating pain tore through his body.

"Noooo!" he growled. He doubled over, clutching his stomach. He stumbled a few steps further, into a chain-link fence. He gripped it, writhing in pain, trying to fight the agony.

But the magic was too strong for him. Thorns sprouted from his grisly face, pierced through his body, slashing his shirt. He howled in torment.

The Charmed Ones, he realized. They're doing this to me! He didn't think they could be so strong so soon. So the legend is true, he thought as the pain wracked his body. Those three sisters are more powerful than any other witch on earth.

One thought helped him bear the agony of their torture. When I finally get them, he vowed, all this power will be mine!

His chest swelled and stretched as if it would burst. Giant rose thorns grew out of his body, pushing through his skin.

Jeremy summoned all his strength to fight the spell. He tried to will the thorns away.

But the pain was overwhelming. The fence slumped under his weight as he fell against it. Blood oozed down his face and chest. He opened his mouth and let out a horrifying howl.

Prue, Piper, and Phoebe leaned over the pot, watching the poppet burn.

What's going to happen? Prue wondered. How could this possibly work? Is burning this silly soap doll really going to keep Jeremy away from us?

BOOM!

Prue jumped as the pot exploded. Flames shot out of the copper bowl. The fire seemed to have a power of its own, a fiercer light than any flames Prue had ever seen.

A moment later the fire died down, and Prue peered into the pot. The poppet had burned to nothing, then disappeared.

"Yes!" Piper cried. "It worked!"

"I thinks she's right," Prue said, amazed and relieved. "It really did!" She reached over and gave Piper a high five. "Are we charmed or what?"

Phoebe leaned over to inspect the copper bowl. She touched the ashes inside.

As soon as she did, a harsh jolt shook her body. She took in a loud gasp of air as she jerked her hand away.

"Phoebe!" Prue cried. "Are you okay?"

Phoebe gazed at her sisters. Prue's heart sank as she saw the terrified expression on Phoebe's face.

"I'm not okay," Phoebe said solemnly. "None of us are. The spell didn't work."

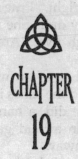

CHAPTER
19

What do you mean, the spell didn't work?" Prue demanded. "I saw those flames. That was not a normal fire!"

"We did everything the book said to do!" Piper cried.

"I know," Phoebe replied. "But I'm sure the spell didn't work."

Prue's heart tightened in her chest. "How do you know?"

"I had a vision," Phoebe explained. "When I touched the pot, I saw Jeremy. He must be a very powerful warlock. We've hurt him, but we haven't killed him."

"You just touched the pot and you saw him?" Piper asked.

Phoebe nodded, her eyes wide with fear. "He's on his way over here."

Prue glanced quickly at her sisters. There was only one thing left to do. "Let's get out of the house!" she cried, springing to her feet.

Prue and her sisters dashed down the staircase and ran straight for the front door. Prue grabbed the handle, threw the door open and screamed.

There, in the doorway, stood Jeremy.

His skin was covered with oozing welts. His clothes were torn and covered with blood. His face twisted in a furious scowl. "Hello, ladies."

Prue, Piper, and Phoebe backed away as Jeremy stepped inside and closed the door.

He pulled the jeweled knife from his pocket and raised it over his head.

Prue stepped in front of Phoebe and Piper, trying to protect her sisters. Together, the three of them inched slowly back. Farther, farther . . .

But with every step they took, Jeremy came closer. His eyes burned red with evil.

Prue stared at Jeremy—at his oozing welts, his blood-covered face, his evil eyes. She stared at him with fury and with power. She stared at him with a force she never knew she possessed. She narrowed her eyes, aiming all her power at Jeremy.

Jeremy's body hurled through the air and slammed against the door with a bang.

"Piper! Phoebe!" she shouted. "Run! Get away! I'll hold him back!"

Prue heard Piper and Phoebe race up the stairs. She backed up a little more, watching Jeremy's every move.

Jeremy pulled himself to his feet. Oh, no, Prue thought. He doesn't look hurt.

"Nice parlor trick, *witch*," he snarled. "You were always the tough one, weren't you, Prue? Didn't even cry at your Mommy's funeral."

"And I won't be crying at yours," Prue snapped.

She concentrated on Jeremy once more, her power flowing through her eyes. Jeremy sailed through the air. He crashed into a wall, smashing the pictures hanging there. Glass shattered and rained on the floor.

Prue didn't waste another second. As soon as Jeremy hit the ground, she turned and raced upstairs to the attic.

Phoebe waited anxiously inside the attic for Prue. "As soon as Prue gets up here, we'll lock the door and block it with furniture," she told Piper.

Phoebe winced when she heard the crash downstairs. "I'm going back down there," she said. "He's too strong for her!"

"No!" Piper cried. "Give her a little more time!"

But it was too hard for Phoebe to wait. Her

adrenaline pumped. She was terrified. "She's been down there too long." She rushed to open the door. "I'm going—" Phoebe stopped.

Prue dashed into the attic and slammed the door behind her. She and Phoebe shoved a dresser against the door.

"You're right," Prue said breathlessly to Phoebe. "Our powers—they're growing."

"Good. We'll need them," Piper said, lodging a table under the doorknob. "Let's put as much against the door as we can!"

"It won't hold Jeremy back," Phoebe said. "But it will buy us a little time."

"Right." Prue helped Piper push a dresser against the door.

Phoebe lifted a chair onto the dresser, and it flew off, crashing to the floor!

The three sisters screamed.

Jeremy's voice—the deep, hollow voice of a demon—boomed outside the door.

He laughed. "Do you think a chair can stop me?"

Phoebe watched as the dresser began to slide away from the door by itself!

"Do you think a dresser can stop me?" Jeremy bellowed.

Phoebe, Prue, and Piper stared helplessly as Jeremy used his power to remove every obstacle that stood between them.

"You witches figured it out yet?" Jeremy cried. "Nothing, *nothing* can stop me!"

The sisters huddled together.

"What do we do?" Piper asked desperately. She glanced around the attic. "There's no way out. We're trapped!"

Phoebe clutched Piper's hand. Her heart raced with terror. Think! she told herself. Think! There must be some way out of this!

Then, in an explosion of power, the door burst open.

Jeremy leaped into the attic room, laughing. He held the golden, jeweled knife in his hand. His head was covered in blood.

Phoebe could see holes in his body where the thorns from their spell had pierced him. Blood oozed from every tear in his skin.

"Come on!" Prue cried, grabbing both sisters by the hand. "We'll face him together!"

Jeremy took a step toward them. He raised the knife.

It can't end like this, Phoebe thought. Melinda, she pleaded silently. You have to help us. Tell me what to do?

But no words came to Phoebe's mind.

Prue let out a loud gasp. "Remember the spirit board!"

That's it! Phoebe thought. "The inscription on the back!" she cried, remembering the night Melinda Warren had appeared. "The power of three!"

"The power of three will set us free," Prue began to chant.

Phoebe and Piper joined in.

"The power of three will set us free."

"No!" Jeremy roared. He clutched his head in pain. The power of the chant hurled him backward. He crashed against the attic door frame.

Something's happening, Phoebe thought. She felt a surge of energy inside her. Something stronger and more electric than she'd ever felt before.

The sisters held hands and kept chanting. "The power of three will set us free."

Jeremy recovered quickly from his fall. He jumped to his feet and flicked his hands at the sisters.

A circle of fire ignited around them, engulfing them. Phoebe gasped. Trapped by swirling flames, she and her sisters could not move out of the tiny, burning circle.

"Come on!" Piper shouted. "We've got to stay together!"

Phoebe huddled closer to her sisters as they continued the chant. "The power of three will set us free." The flames crackled and licked at their skin, but didn't burn them.

Scowling with frustration, Jeremy waved his hands at them again.

The fire changed into a swirling vortex of dust.

Phoebe choked for air. Grit blew into her eyes and into her lungs. Coughing, she broke the chant.

Piper stopped, too, gasping for breath.

Phoebe felt Prue grip her hand tighter. "The power of three will set us free!" she cried.

Still choking on the dust, Phoebe and Piper joined in again.

A bolt of lightning flashed through the attic window. It split the sky. Thunder shook the house.

It's working, Phoebe thought. Our chant is calling on some kind of power—some power outside ourselves.

The cyclone of dust swirled harder and faster. The gusts of wind blew Phoebe's hair straight up. But Phoebe could feel it moving away, moving toward Jeremy.

"The power of three will set us free! The power of three will set us free!"

Phoebe watched Jeremy closely as she chanted. The vortex swirled around him, pulling at his body, tearing at his skin, ripping him apart.

The thunder and lightning grew louder and stronger, as Phoebe and her sisters continued the chant—so loud and so strong as the storm raged inside the house.

Jeremy writhed in pain as the wind and dust disfigured him, forcing his body to take the form of the cyclone—until Phoebe could barely see any part of him.

"The power of three will set us free! The power of three will set us free!" the sisters shouted.

A howl sounded from the vortex. Then an enormous snake-like creature emerged from the center.

Phoebe gasped at the sight. The creature had Jeremy's face!

"I am not the only one!" he shouted. "I am one of millions! In places you can't even imagine! In forms you would never believe! We are hell on earth!"

"THE POWER OF THREE WILL SET US FREE!" The sisters cried louder, faster, as hard as they could. "THE POWER OF THREE WILL SET US FREE!"

"You'll never be safe!" Jeremy bellowed. "And you'll never be free!"

He gave one last roar. Then he exploded into nothingness.

The hurricane of dust died down and disappeared.

The thunder and lightning stopped.

Phoebe, Piper, and Prue found themselves standing alone in the attic, holding hands.

Phoebe tried to catch her breath, amazed at what had just happened.

"The power of three," Prue said.

The three sisters collapsed together on the floor, hugging one another.

We're safe, Phoebe told herself. But for how long?

CHAPTER
20

Prue rolled over on her bed the next morning, feeling relaxed. She was surprised at how well she had slept the night before and at how rested she felt. Then the previous night's events flooded back to her. She stirred, troubled.

My life is different now, Prue realized as she threw off the covers and got out of bed. It will never be the same again.

I used to worry about my job and my love life, she thought. And my sisters.

Now I've got to think about a whole universe of evil. About warlocks trying to kill me. About how to use my powers for good. And I *still* have to worry about my job, my love life, and my sisters. She laughed.

Prue took a quick shower and dressed in a

red T-shirt and denim capri pants. Then she skipped down the stairs to get the paper. Piper and Phoebe were still asleep.

She opened the front door and stepped outside, reaching for the newspaper on the welcome mat.

"Good morning."

Prue looked up to find Andy standing at the foot of the steps.

He was dressed for work, in a dark suit, white shirt, and blue tie. He started up the steps, carrying a tall paper cup of coffee.

"This is a surprise," Prue said. She was glad to see him. He's not a warlock, she reminded herself—probably not, anyway. After what had happened with Jeremy, Prue knew she'd never be completely sure about anything ever again. She had to hone her instincts and learn to trust them. And when it came to Andy, her instincts told her to relax.

I've treated him terribly, Prue realized. No wonder he acted strangely around me—I was behaving like a lunatic. She knew she had to apologize to him, but how? How could she explain why she acted the way she did?

Prue sat on the top step, holding the paper in her lap. Andy settled beside her.

"What are you doing here so early?" she asked.

"Well . . ." He hesitated. "I came to see if you wanted to have dinner with me tonight. And the next night. And the next. Unless, of course, you're afraid."

"Afraid of what?" she asked.

"You tell me," Andy said. "You left in such a hurry yesterday. I couldn't help wondering if I'd done something wrong."

"No, Andy." Prue struggled to explain. "You haven't done anything wrong. Not at all." She stared at her feet. She could feel his eyes on her, watching her, trying to understand.

"Well, good," he said at last. "So what do you say about dinner tonight? Francesca's? Eight o'clock?"

Prue wanted to say yes. She opened her mouth to speak, but something stopped her. She wanted to have dinner with him. She really did. But what would it mean? What could it lead to?

So Andy *wasn't* a warlock, but Prue still had a big problem. She wasn't the girl Andy had known years ago. She was a witch now. Her life was never going to be the same.

I can't exactly tell him I'm a witch, she thought. And if I can't be honest with him— what kind of relationship could we have?

"You're hesitating," Andy said. His smile wilted.

"Yes," Prue said, feeling a little sad. "But it's not what you think. My life . . . it's gotten a little complicated. I care about you a lot. But I—I don't think I can be in a relationship right now. Can I call you?"

"Sure." Andy reached into his jacket pocket and pulled out a business card. He stood up and handed it to her.

"Call me any time," he said. "If you ever need anything . . . Take care, Prue."

"Bye, Andy."

She watched sadly as he walked to his car.

The door opened behind her. Piper and Phoebe stepped outside, each dressed in sweats for a morning run.

Piper and Phoebe stared curiously at Andy's car as he drove away.

Phoebe turned to Piper and said, "I told you I heard a man's voice."

"What did he want?" Piper asked Prue.

"He asked me to have dinner with him tonight," Prue replied.

"Great!" Phoebe cried. "Now that we know he's probably not a warlock you can go with my blessing."

Prue wrinkled her nose.

"What's wrong?" Piper asked Prue. "Didn't you say yes?"

"I started to say yes, but I stopped," Prue answered. "He's a great guy. He deserves to be with someone who can be open with him. I can't."

"I don't think it's a good idea to be too open with men, anyway," Phoebe joked. "Witch or no witch."

"I'm serious," Prue said. "I wonder if I can

get involved with a guy at all anymore. I mean, do witches date?"

Piper and Phoebe joined their sister on the top step.

"Not only do they date," Piper said cheerfully, "they usually get the best guys."

Phoebe laughed and added, "And the best jewelry."

Prue frowned. She still felt troubled.

"But how will we ever feel safe?" she asked. "How will we know who to trust?"

"We can't suspect every guy we meet," Piper said. "We'll have to use our instincts. Maybe, after a while, we'll know how to spot a warlock a mile away."

Prue shook her head. "Even so, everything's going to be different from now on."

"At least our lives won't be boring," Phoebe said.

"But they'll never be the same," Prue protested.

"This is a *bad* thing?" Phoebe joked.

"No, but it could be a big problem," Prue replied, thinking of the secret they had to carry with them.

"Prue's right," Piper said. "What are we going to do?"

Phoebe grinned mischievously. "What *can't* we do?"

Prue turned and headed inside the house. Piper and Phoebe followed her.

"We're going to be careful," Prue said as she walked through the front door. "We're going to be wise. And we're going to stick together."

The three sisters stood inside the foyer now. Prue glanced at the open door behind her, then at Piper and Phoebe. Why not? she wondered with a devious smile.

She nodded her head at the door. Magically, it swung shut.

Piper grinned at her. "This should be interesting."